BOUNCER'S BATTLE

Gus Beaumont Thrillers
Book One

Tony Rea

Also in the Gus Beaumont Series

Bouncer's Blenheim

BOUNCER'S BATTLE

Published by Sapere Books.

24 Trafalgar Road, Ilkley, LS29 8HH

saperebooks.com

ISBN: 978-0-85495-275-5

Dedicated to Ian Woodason sometime Adjutant of the Keynsham Light Horse, who tragically died whilst this book was being written.

ACKNOWLEDGEMENTS

My heartfelt thanks go to Roger King, Major Matthew Rea and my wife Jane for reading and critically commenting on the text. Thanks also to everyone at the Ivybridge writing group; their wise observations have strengthened the story massively. Agnieszka Treleaven helped with the Polish dialogue and, as always, Amy Durant and the team at Sapere Books have contributed their experience and professionalism. Thank you all.

"The gratitude of every home in our island goes out to the British airmen who, undaunted by odds, unwearied in their constant challenge and mortal danger, are turning the tide of the World War…

Never in the field of human conflict was so much owed by so many to so few."

Winston Churchill, August 1940

PART ONE: THE SUMMER BEFORE THE WAR

CHAPTER 1

May 1939

It was Gus Beaumont's first solo flight. The gleaming, yellow biplane stood at the leeward end of the grass strip. Gus smiled contentedly as he gazed at it. It was an Avro 504 model N, two-seat training aircraft, redesigned after the Great War as a basic trainer for the RAF. With its hundred and sixty horsepower Armstrong Siddeley Lynx engine, the 504N was very much superior to the wartime variants, and the West Suffolk Aero Club was lucky to have two of them.

"Ready?" called his instructor, Larry Hislop.

"Ready as I'll ever be."

"Don't worry, you'll nail it, son! Just go easy on those landings, hey?"

Gus glanced at his instructor. He guessed that Hislop didn't want the maiden solo of his protégé spoilt by any mishaps. He didn't want to see a repeat of the many heavy landings early in his basic training.

Gus was a natural flyer. He wasn't, however, the best at landing. The first time he brought a 504 down to land on the grassy strip at the club, he came down heavily on three points and tore the tail skid off the Avro. The second time he took it too easy and the plane bumped heavily, recoiled back into the air, repeated the whole thing and eventually thumped down on the third bounce. It earned Gus the nickname of 'Bouncer'.

He smiled. "Don't worry, Larry. I'll go easy."

"Look, Bouncer. You're already a good pilot and can only get better so long as you don't kill yourself landing. You just need to calm down a little, lad. Don't be so hasty. Especially on final approaches, got it?"

"I've got it, Larry."

Gus climbed into the 504's open cockpit, strapped in and checked the flying controls and cockpit switches.

"Prime the engine!" he shouted.

The engineers used a syringe to inject a small amount of fuel through the exhaust valve of each cylinder. Gus checked that the chocks were in position and that two men were holding back the aircraft by the tailskid. Then he set the block tube lever to a position on the graduated scale that he knew from experience roughly equated to satisfactory low power. Not easy.

After turning on the ignition, Gus called contact and the groundcrew took hold of the polished, laminated propellor and swung it. The 504 had a large prop and a relatively heavy engine, so this wasn't an easy job. One, two swings and the engine fired, running on the injected prime charge. As the charge was used up, the engine began to stop and Gus eased the fine adjustment lever forward to catch the engine. The Armstrong Siddeley Lynx thundered into action, sending smoke streaming off into the slight breeze.

This was the difficult stage, playing with the fuel mix to ensure the engine neither cut out nor overran. Gus knew that the 504 must be airborne within two and a half minutes of first starting the engine or it might overheat with possible damage.

"Chocks away!" he shouted, waving to Hislop. He gunned the engine, opening the throttle full, then sent the Avro rushing along the strip into the wind. Within seconds he was rising up into the sky. Once airborne, he flew at full power and he was able to relax a little, gazing down on the rolling greenery of Sussex and the blue sea in the distance.

After fifteen minutes, Gus was lining up his approach, flying into the wind and reducing his speed to just fifty knots. As he did so, he closed off the fine adjustment, cutting the fuel supply off. The prop and engine continued to rotate due to the slipstream, but produced zero power. Once certain of landing within the airfield boundary, Gus side-slipped the Avro to increase the rate of descent. The aircraft touched down perfectly on three points and stopped in a very short space.

Hislop stood, pipe in mouth, clapping. "First class, lad. First bloody class."

For the past two years, Gus had been studying History at the University of Oxford, while learning to fly planes in his spare time. By the end of June, exams were finished, the results had been published and the students' bags were packed. The Trinity term had ended, and the students were looking forward to a holiday. Gus 'Bouncer' Beaumont had built up his solo hours to just short of thirty, mostly in Avro 504s but also half a dozen in the club's Hawker Hart. Now, he was waking up hungover and bleary-eyed following a last Saturday night on the town in Oxford.

Despite a thick head, he hurried to organise himself. He rushed his breakfast, knowing he must not miss the train that would take him home to his family. He arrived on the platform with ninety seconds to spare, only to discover the train was half an hour late. He bought himself a cup of coffee and a newspaper while he waited. For once the headline was not dominated by news of events in Europe, East Africa, or Manchuria. Four bombs had exploded in London's theatreland, causing at least twenty injuries and mass panic among Saturday night crowds. *It must be the IRA again*, Gus thought.

Eventually his train turned up and Gus snoozed on the uneventful ride to Winchester. As he stepped down from the carriage at Cheesehill Station, he took a couple of long breaths of the fresh Hampshire air to clear his head.

The platform was dotted with people. Some, like him, were arriving. Others were waiting expectantly for loved ones. Several were departing, luggage around them, with family or friends tearfully waving them off. He saw his mother, Magda Beaumont. She was dressed in a pretty, light-green summer suit and matching hat, with a handbag over one arm.

"Gus!" she shouted over the noise of the engine, waving frantically, "Gustaw!"

Gus picked up his suitcase and walked towards her. They met somewhere near the middle of the platform as a whistle sounded. He kissed her cheeks as, with a great belch of steam, the train pulled out of the station to resume its journey to Southampton.

"Good to see you, Mother," said Gus.

"Welcome home," said Magda. "I thought you would have travelled first class."

"*Nie*, I'm saving money for my holiday."

They walked in silence to the gleaming, black Austin Windsor saloon that stood waiting for them outside the station.

"Good morning to you, young Mr Beaumont, and very good to see you back," said the chauffeur, Albert Cross, as Gus climbed into the car.

"Hello, Albert, nice to see you again."

The chauffeur, who had been in service since Gus was a young child, closed the door behind him.

As they drove off, Gus asked, "How is Father?"

"Well," Magda replied. "You'll soon see him for yourself."

Gus saw the beginnings of tears in his mother's eyes as she searched in her handbag for her cigarette case and lighter. As she offered him a cigarette, he noticed how badly some of her fingernails had been chewed.

"You know I don't smoke them," he said.

There wasn't time for Gus to do more than exchange pleasantries with his father. He slept for much of the afternoon, and that evening the Beaumonts had company. The Blagdons, who lived a short drive away, and Gerald Palmer arrived for dinner shortly after six.

Lionel Beaumont coughed and cleared his throat, then he introduced the Blagdons to Palmer. "Meet Gerald Palmer," he said. "You'll know him as our Member of Parliament, but you might not know that Gerald is a descendant of the..." He started coughing again. As he coughed, he pulled a pale blue handkerchief from his pocket, with which he tried to smother his face. Eventually he cleared his throat and spat something into the handkerchief. Gus noticed the redness and looked at his mother. He thought he saw her nod.

The old man steadied himself and went on, "...the ... the biscuit magnates of Reading."

"Pleased to meet you, sir," said Mr Blagdon.

"Gerald's biscuits sustained the nation, you know," said Lionel. "Scott took them with him to the Antarctic, and there's many a soldier who's been glad of them in the trenches."

Blagdon and Palmer dominated what conversation there was around the dinner table. Blagdon twittered on, first about biscuits then the Newbury races, and Palmer confused everyone with his accounts of Eastern Orthodox writings. Gus noticed that they chose to ignore or avoid any conversation about the impending crisis in Europe.

Their meal began with pigeon breasts on buttered toast, followed by lamb cutlets and roasted vegetables. For dessert, a raspberry fool was offered — in his honour, no doubt. As usual, there was good claret on the table throughout.

After dinner, Gus sat with his father and the other men in the smoking room. Appreciation of fine cigars and good port seemed to be the only things they all had in common, but Gus couldn't help thinking the fug wasn't good for his father's lungs.

When the Blagdons and Palmer had left and Magda had taken her customary early night, Lionel beckoned Gus over. "Do you have time for a chat for before bed?" he asked.

They went back to the smoking room.

"I got the impression you didn't much care for Gerald Palmer," said Lionel.

"I'm sorry. Was it so obvious?"

"He wouldn't have noticed. Blagdon neither. I think Mrs Blagdon did, though — that's why she kept smiling at you. She found it amusing."

"Well, no harm done then," said Gus.

His father poured them each another glass of port. "You are determined to go to Poland this year?"

"It might be the last chance for me to visit again. A war looks likely, you know…"

"Oh, don't I know it! We all know. Yes, there is a war coming, and I shall be no damned use in it! Harris gave me no more than three months when I saw him in March. I'm already on borrowed time, son."

He took a long drag on the cigar. "Look, it's not that I want you to stay here because of me. I'm ready to go, face my maker as they say. It's enough that you came to visit me before going off on your travels. But your mother, she has no-one else."

"I know, Father, and I do feel guilty about it. But..." Gus paused to think.

"You know your mother," said Lionel. "She ... she doesn't exactly fit in with the local community."

"Because she's Polish?"

"Partly, but Winchester can cope with that."

"Not because she is Jewish? Surely...?"

"Of course not! Most of the Rosens were only ever secular Jews, anyway. Your grandfather may have made his fortune from trading around central Europe prior to the Great War, but he rarely went near a synagogue. Cousin Staś's parents were no different. Uncle Theodore was the only Orthodox one amongst them. He ended up moving to the Holy Land — Palestine."

"Then why?"

"From the first time I met your mother, I was infatuated. It was an early summer soiree — May, I believe — held at the ambassador's residence in Warsaw, and she looked stunning. A diamond amongst jewels. But I had no idea of her background, her friends and associates — not that it would have made any difference. Your mother is, er, rather liberal in her political views. Did you know that as a young woman your mother mixed with Rozalia Luksenburg?"

"Who?"

"Oh, it doesn't matter. Just to say, your mother is ... how do I put it? She's like you, a bit of a liberal. More liberal than most of the ladies roundabout. And she has always been outspoken. On occasion, it causes..."

"You're saying she's an outsider?" asked Gus.

"Let's just say there are few liberally minded and secular Jewish Poles in Winchester," said his father. "It's as simple as that and because of it, she has few friends."

They smoked in silence for a while.

"But none of this helps us, Gustaw. Why must you travel to Poland? Why is it so urgent?"

"You know I always spend my summers in Lublin. Of course, I want to go back — visit Staś now that he's an instructor…"

"Stanislaw Rosen is so important?"

"Staś, yes. I want to go flying and…" He paused, considering what to say.

"And?" Lionel eyed him. "Perhaps there's a girl involved?"

"You guessed," Gus said, eventually.

"This girl, is she beautiful?"

"Very beautiful."

"If it is a girl that draws you to Poland and if she is even half as beautiful as your mother, then you may travel with my blessing. What's more, I shall make you a promise."

"A promise?"

"Yes, I refuse to die until your return."

Gus retired to bed that night happy that he had his father's approval for a trip to Poland — not that anything would have stopped him. He was happier still that he had kept secret the other reason for his urgency to travel abroad.

CHAPTER 2

The previous month, while still at university, Gus had had a strange encounter with a man he'd never seen before. Wing Commander Sir Alexander Peacock had insisted their meeting was an accident, but Gus thought it was nothing of the sort. He was sure he'd been targeted.

Following an evening on the river, Gus was enjoying a drink in the bar of the Turf Tavern. Once most of the other students had departed, Peacock approached the bar with an empty glass in his hand and bumped into him. Gus jolted and spilt some of his beer.

"So sorry, old boy! Please let me get you a drink, would you?"

"Don't mind if you do. Mine's a pint of bitter."

The barman pulled the pump handle steadily. A fountain of amber-coloured ale flowed into the tall glass. He stopped short of a pint to allow the liquor to settle. Whilst the beer was resting, a white froth forming on the top of the tall glass, he poured Peacock a shot of gin.

Peacock turned to Gus, a quizzical look on his face. "I say, you're Lionel Beaumont's lad, aren't you? Must be! Absolute spitting image of your father."

They sat down together, drinks in hand. Gus eyed the well-dressed and properly spoken stranger, who he put much closer to his father's age than his own.

"I hear Lionel's not too rosy these days."

"No. He's very poorly, I'm afraid."

"Ah. Sorry to hear that."

"So, how do you know my father?"

"I worked with him in Poland, in the early 1920s."

"At the embassy?"

"Not exactly."

"Where, then?"

Peacock ignored the question. "I suppose you speak Polish — good Polish?"

"Look," said Gus, "what's all this about?"

Without answering, Peacock finished his drink and took a card out of his jacket pocket. Then he rose from the table, thrusting the card into Gus's hand. "Meet me for lunch next Saturday and I can explain everything. There may be a job you could do. A special task, for king and country. It's, erm, very hush, hush, if you follow me. One p.m. sharp. Don't be late."

Peacock was gone before he could say anything, but Gus was already too fascinated not to go. He looked at the card:

Wing Commander Sir Alexander Peacock
The Royal Air Force Club
128 Piccadilly

Having taken the train from Oxford to London, Gus walked from Paddington to Piccadilly the following Saturday. He saw sandbags up against public buildings, workmen and soldiers digging slit-trenches and gangs of men putting in the preparations for barrage balloon stations. England was on a war footing following the Czech crisis of the previous year. On his final day of classes prior to exams, Gus had watched in sadness as a military convoy trundled along the High. It must have been a mile long.

It was all the fault of the old Tories in government — Baldwin, Chamberlain, and the others and their defeatist policy. Chamberlain had been right to remind the nation that war was a terrible thing, but what was the point in trying to appease the dictators? When Hitler had sent his troops into the Rhineland, Gus had been appalled that the British and French did nothing. After all, it was a blatant breach of an international treaty. Then there was the dreadful deal at Munich last year that had left the Czechs completely in the lurch and allowed Hitler to seize the rest of Czechoslovakia.

Poland, surely, was next on Hitler's list of land-grabs.

Gus arrived at the Club just before twelve thirty, and a white-jacketed steward took him to a large reception room. There were two men waiting for him, both in RAF uniform.

Peacock stepped forward to greet him. "Allow me to introduce Squadron Leader Taylor," he said.

He shook Taylor by the hand, finding his grip rather weak and insincere.

"Piotr Taylor," announced the squadron leader. "Please sit down. I understand you speak Polish?"

Gus sat down as invited. "Yes, my mother is Polish. She often speaks the language to me when we are alone."

"I expect that your reading and writing is just as good as your speech?"

"They are both adequate. I went to school there for a while."

"Yes, we are aware of that," said Taylor. "And we know you have visited your Polish cousins every summer since 1930. Time for luncheon, I think," he said.

The three of them went to lunch. As they ate, the conversation continued. Peacock and Taylor went on to outline what they wanted Gus to do.

"We need you to have a difficult conversation with your cousin, Flying Officer Stanislaw Rosen — he is posted to the air force academy at the present time. Correct?" asked Taylor.

Gus was surprised that they knew so much about his cousin Stanislaw as well as himself. "You seem to know everything. It's not for me to contradict you."

"You have to tell him that when war breaks out between Poland and the Nazis, the French will do nothing. Nothing, tell him."

"And without the French," added Peacock, "neither will we British do anything."

"Hold on, hold on," said Gus. "Why don't you communicate this through the normal channels?"

"We simply can't," said Peacock. "The Poles are in the middle of negotiations to purchase a number of Hawker Hurricanes from us. We can hardly send Sir Howard over from the Warsaw Embassy to tell Składkowski that the British won't stand by him, can we?"

Gus could think of nothing to say. They had everything, every detail sewn up.

"Our intelligence suggests that Stalin will use a German invasion of Poland as an excuse to move on the Poles from the east," Peacock went on, now dominating the conversation. "Poland is bound to collapse within days. It's inevitable — they needn't feel embarrassed about it, but in the longer run Britain and France will fight and will need trained pilots."

"Tell Flying Officer Rosen that as many pilots and ground crew as possible must get out of Poland," said Taylor.

"They can fly out, drive out, walk out, whatever, but they must leave. They should then make their way to France or Britain," said Peacock. "If they can get to Romania, the British Embassy there will help. They will have a plan to carry them safely through Romania and Bulgaria to Greece, and from there to western Europe."

"But why Staś? He's nowhere near the top of the Polish forces."

"There is an instructor at the air force academy who has contacts in high places. Captain Witold Nowacki," said Taylor. "You will need to be insistent with Flying Officer Rosen. Rosen must pass on this information. He must make Nowacki understand just how serious the situation is."

"Yes, it is vital!" agreed Peacock. "Now, recite to me the entire message and we'll make sure you've got it all correct, shall we?"

Gus repeated what he had been told.

Taylor stood, his meal hardly touched. "It's time that I left," he said. "I have another meeting to attend."

Once he was out of earshot, Peacock said, "You fly yourself, don't you?"

"Yes. At the club in West Suffolk."

"How many solo hours?"

"Twenty-odd, mostly in Avros, but half a dozen in Hawker Harts."

"Ever thought about joining the Royal Auxiliaries?" asked Peacock. "We'll soon need lots of pilots, you know. Lots!"

CHAPTER 3

Less than a week after visiting his parents in Winchester, and a month after his meeting with Peacock and Taylor, Gus took a sleeper berth on the Compagnie Internationale des Wagons-Lits' Nord Express. The Express service was by no means cheap, but it departed from Calais at a reasonable time of day and was a convenient way of journeying to Warsaw. The train was run by a French company, and so the service, food and wine were excellent.

Unable to settle, Gus alighted at Paris for a wander around the platform. The mood didn't seem like that in London; he didn't sense that people were preparing for a war.

Later, at the Franco-German border, there was a knock on his cabin door and stern-faced officials entered.

"*Reisepass, bitte*!" one of them demanded.

Gus handed over his passport. A guard scrutinised it and, in a harsh voice, asked in German, "Herr Beaumont, what is your destination?"

"I'm visiting friends in Poland," he replied, also in German, "not that it is any of your business."

The official glared at him, thrust back his passport, and stomped off.

When the guards were out of earshot, a steward said, "Excuse me, sir. You are better off just playing their game. Power goes to their heads. Annoy them, and they can make your journey rather difficult."

"They seem to get more bullish and authoritative each year I make this journey."

"Yes, they have become worse since..." The steward suddenly shut up and looked around.

"You mean since Hitler came to power, don't you? Nobody's listening; it's quite all right."

"You just never know these days."

The following morning, the Nord Express approached the border with Poland. Gus was seated in the dining car for an early breakfast, drinking coffee and enjoying delicious French pastries. He was entertained by the conversation of an elderly couple.

The man looked out of the carriage window. "All this is Germany, you know. This damned so-called Polish corridor — " he waved towards the countryside speeding by — "it was stolen, stolen I say! German land pilfered to give the bloody Poles access to the Baltic."

"Yes, Herman, but do be a little quieter," said the woman.

"Quiet? Why should I be quiet? It's left German-speaking people in the east cut off. They're completely isolated from their motherland."

"Yes, Herman."

"And Danzig a 'free city'? The bloody Poles are already calling it Gdansk! Is this what our Willy died for?"

The old woman said nothing; she just stared down into her lap.

Gus noticed the old man was wearing a Nazi Party pin badge on the lapel of his jacket. He understood that Germans resented the Polish corridor and other aspects of the 1919 treaty, but he never believed they would fight to regain the land — until now.

The election of Adolf Hitler had changed everything. He had stirred up anger with his talk of back-stabbing at Versailles and the need for '*Lebensraum*' — a living space for ethnic Germans. He had spread hate with his horrific scapegoating of the Jews.

Gus looked away. He opened his book, Trevelyan's *The Recreations of an Historian*, and sat reading for the rest of the journey to Warsaw.

There was no girl waiting for Gus in Poland. Once in Warsaw, he had a quick walk around outside the station, then took the train to Lublin. Once there, he spotted his cousin waiting for him on the arrival concourse.

"Staś!" he shouted, to attract his attention. "Staś!"

Stanislaw was four years older than Gus. He was tall and blond, and had a habit of kissing ladies' hands when he met them. Dressed in the uniform of a Porucznik — or Lieutenant — in the Polish Air Force, Gus noticed that Staś was attracting the gazes of women passing by.

They greeted each other with embraces and a kiss on the cheek.

"How are you, Gustaw?"

"Better for seeing you."

"And you brought your licence?"

"Just as you suggested," replied Gus.

"Then we travel straight to the academy. There's the car — jump in." Staś pointed to a large, four-door, five-seater saloon painted maroon and beige, with wide running boards and a large spare wheel on the right-hand side.

Gus thought it stunning. "Wow!" he exclaimed. "What a car, Staś! What is it?"

"It's a Polski-Fiat 'Mazur'. Father bought it this year; it has the latest two-litre Fiat engine. Come on!"

Off they went, navigating the streets of Lublin. As they emerged from the city, the roads opened up and Staś, clearly showing off to his English cousin, began to put the car through its paces, smiling and laughing as he sped through the open countryside.

"It's lovely to drive, Gustaw," said Staś, "a really smooth four-speed box."

"You sound like a motor car salesman, Staś. But I'll indulge you. How fast will it go?"

"The manual says it can do one hundred and ten."

"Kilometres?" asked Gus.

"What else? I've only managed a hundred, though. Do you want a try?"

"Why not?"

Staś stopped the Mazur and they swapped seats.

On a long, straight stretch of road, Gus gunned the large, powerful Fiat engine. His face contorted in concentration, he tried to better his cousin's top speed but had to slow down as the road ran out.

"You win, Staś!" he conceded.

As they carried on towards the air force academy at Dęblin, with nobody to overhear, Gus decided it was the ideal opportunity to talk to his cousin.

"Staś," he said, "I need to speak to you about something very important."

"Why be serious when we're having such fun?"

"Because it is serious! You have to listen carefully. Listen to the whole story from start to finish, then you can ask questions. I'll do my best to answer, understood?"

"Understood," said his cousin.

First, he told Staś about his 'chance' meeting with Peacock in the Turf and the invitation to the RAF Club in Piccadilly.

"So, you went to London for lunch with a stranger?"

"A stranger who knew, or claimed to know, my father, yes. Look, do you know an officer called Witold Nowacki?"

"Nowacki? Yes, I know him."

Gus then told his cousin about his conversation with Peacock and Taylor and related the message as instructed.

"There you are, Staś, and now you must give this same message to Captain Nowacki."

Staś was silent for a while. "But our government has ordered Hurricanes from Britain," he protested.

"And have they arrived?" asked Gus.

"Not yet. This Squadron Leader Taylor, can you describe him?"

"Tall, thin face, striking hazel eyes, moustaches."

"Did he have a weak handshake?"

"Yes. You know him?"

"Piotr Krawiec," announced Staś, convincingly. "I don't know him personally, but I've met him. Krawiec was a pilot in the war. After, he went into the Civil Service, foreign department. He's obviously in the London Embassy. I will deliver the message, Gustaw. Trust me. But now — we fly!"

They had driven through the gates of the Polish Air Force Academy at Dęblin, and Staś stopped the car beside two PZL P-7 fighter planes.

"They're both fuelled up and ready to go," said Staś. "Let's get you dressed, then I'll take you through the controls."

Soon the two cousins were flying high above the Polish landscape. Gus soon got the hang of the P-7, although it was the first time he had flown a mono-wing aircraft. The high-mounted gull-shaped wing gave him a fantastic field of view. Following his cousin, Gus found the P-7 light on the controls and agile, and he soon found himself diving and banking at severe aeroplane to ground angles.

As the P-7s were not fitted with radios, Staś had to use hand signals to tell Gus what to do. Now he was frantically signalling for Gus to come down. *Right*, thought Gus, *time to find out how fast she is.*

Staś had told him that P-7s had a top speed of three hundred and seventeen kilometres per hour, which Gus estimated at about a hundred and seventy knots, just a little faster than the Hawker Harts he was used to. He put the P-7 into a steep dive, and soon the wind buffeted around his head as he gathered speed. The air speed indicator told him the ground was approaching at three hundred kilometres per hour, but still Gus carried on.

Staś was circling at five thousand feet. Gus pictured him watching in disbelief.

The ground was coming closer and closer. *I'm never going to get to top speed*, Gus thought. *Time to pull out.* He pulled back on the control column and felt the incredible G-force pushing him into his seat, but the P-7 didn't respond. There was sweat running down his face. *Think. Think, man*, he thought. *What were you taught? Ease the stick into neutral; look for the nearest horizon. Roll out of the dive towards it.* With five hundred feet to go, the P-7 began to respond, enabling Gus to roll out of the dive. He thanked God that there were no trees around.

He levelled out and looked for Staś. There he was, circling above and waving for Gus to go back to the airfield. Gus landed first, bouncing the P-7 on the grassy strip then taxiing back to the hangars. His cousin followed him down with a perfect approach and smooth touchdown.

Once he stopped the P-7 and the ground crew had the chocks in place, Staś cut the engine. He jumped out of his cockpit and sprinted over to Gus's plane with an angry look on his face.

"What do you think you were doing, man?" he asked, furiously.

"Sorry. I thought you were indicating for me to try her out in a dive."

"No, I was telling you to land. You almost lost her. You know that? The bloody undercarriage almost grounded! What's more, you could have killed yourself, you idiot!"

Gus was silent. Staś was right. It had been a foolish thing to do, especially in an unfamiliar kite.

Gus unstrapped and clambered out of the P-7. "You're correct, of course," he said, shamefaced. "Sorry, Staś."

"Bit of a heavy landing, too," he said with half a smile.

Gus smiled back. "The boys at the club nickname me Bouncer," he said. "But come on, Staś, it wasn't that bad! Anyway, I'll soon be landing Hurricanes or Spitfires. When I get home, I'm going to follow Peacock's suggestion and apply to join the Royal Auxiliary Air Force."

Staś slapped his cousin across the shoulders. "With landings like that," he said, "the RAF won't let you close to their fighters. They're much too precious. I bet you'll be confined to those bloody indestructible Lysanders! Anyway, what's the Auxiliary Air Force?"

"It's all to do with social class," replied Gus, trying to explain. "The saying goes like this: a regular is an officer trying to be a gentleman. An auxiliary is a gentleman trying to be an officer. Then there's the volunteer reservists: they're new money trying their damned hardest to be both!"

CHAPTER 4

Lionel kept the promise he made to his son. He died at home, Magda and Gus by his side, a few weeks after Gus's return from Poland. It was 17th September and it brought double misfortune for Magda. Her husband died on the same day that Stalin chose to invade eastern Poland.

Not that the Soviet invasion came as any surprise. A fortnight earlier, as German troops invaded western Poland, all three Beaumonts sat in silence, staring at the wireless that sat on the sideboard in Lionel's bedroom. There was an expectant hush as they waited for Neville Chamberlain to speak. Eventually, the wireless crackled to life, and they strained to hear what the Prime Minister had to say.

"I am speaking to you from the Cabinet Room at 10 Downing Street," Chamberlain announced. "This morning the British ambassador in Berlin handed the German Government a final note stating that unless we heard from them by 11 o'clock that they were prepared at once to withdraw their troops from Poland, a state of war would exist between us. I have to tell you now that no such undertaking has been received, and that consequently this country is at war with Germany."

"Turn it off!" said Magda, angrily.

Gus turned the black knob so that the sound cracked and died away.

Magda took a cigarette and lighter from her handbag. "The Russians will invade soon," she said as she tried but failed to light the cigarette. "Poland is finished!"

"Poland is finished and I'm finished," said Lionel, and the emotion launched him into another fit of coughing.

Magda Beaumont walked into St Peter's Roman Catholic Church behind her late husband's coffin. She had refused to wear black; she was instead dressed in a subdued shade of red and walked on the arm of her son. The church was packed. On the way out, she forced a smile for members of Lionel's family who were seated towards the front. Staś was there, too, but nobody else from Magda's side of the family had managed to get out of Poland. She spotted the Blagdons and Gerald Palmer further to the rear of the church. Gus noticed Wing Commander Sir Alex Peacock sitting just behind Palmer, but he didn't attend the wake.

It was early evening by the time the guests had departed.

"It's been a difficult day. I am going to bed early, if you will excuse me," declared Magda.

"Of course, Mother."

"Tell me what it was like, Staś," said Gus as they sat with a bottle of reserve tawny port.

Staś said nothing at first. He simply stared at his cousin, but as they drank he gradually opened up and explained how Poland lost the short war and how he and thousands of others escaped.

"It was terrible!" said Staś. "The Nazis destroyed most of our air force on the ground. We had no chance."

He took the decanter and poured more port for Gus and himself. He then took a long, slow sip before he continued.

"Of course, we wanted to fight. We were ready and waiting for them. We just didn't realise how…" Staś seemed close to tears. He took another sip of his wine. "On paper, our army looked formidable. Three hundred thousand men and two million reservists. The fourth largest army in Europe. We had tanks, but they were mostly old, small, slow and poorly armed. Just mobile machine guns to support the infantry. And, yes, we still had our splendid cavalry. Our generals expected the German infantry to march as they did in 1914 and supposed our cavalry would be able to fend off attacks by mounting rapid thrusts over Poland's roadless plains. Shit!" Staś poured more port, and Gus knew they would both have filthy hangovers the next day. But this was Staś's tale and Gus wanted to listen.

"Almost two million Nazi troops — two million, Gus! And hundreds of tanks. What's more, their tactics were so much better. Believe me, if we are hit by them in France in the same way, they will murder us! Their tanks come in front, with their infantry in support. The German bombers supply supporting heavy firepower. They operate the total opposite way to which our military planners — and yours, I fear — conceptualise warfare."

"Sounds bloody awful," said Gus.

"The Luftwaffe came first. Their planes were faster, better armed, and could fly higher, than our … our relics! Our cockpits filled with smoke from our machine guns so we couldn't see. Once I saw a pilot crash and die because the interrupter mechanism failed and he shot off his own propeller. In a Hurricane or Spitfire, or even a French fighter, you're much more competitive, but you're still vulnerable because they hit you without warning. On the ground, if they can. At Dęblin, the first we knew about it was when Witold 'Tunio' Nowacki and a cadet were practising in P-7s and a Messerschmitt 109 got in between them. Tunio thought the cadet had opened fire on him — he was lucky not to be hit. I told him he should go to church and light a candle.

"I transferred to the Kościuszko Squadron, part of the Warsaw Pursuit Brigade. Our job was the defence of the capital. The squadron was briefed that we had a chance, but only if we could get above them, dive and get close, very close, before opening fire. We hurled ourselves into the attack. On that first day we shot down six bombers but lost three Polish fighters. The Luftwaffe was relentless, Gus. Wave after wave of bombers were set on Warsaw; those days are still a blur. No sooner had we returned from one sortie than we were scrambled again. In the end, the task became impossible. Polish fighters, even the P-11s, can barely catch a Heinkel bomber and the Germans had a four to one advantage in numbers of planes. We did what we could. If only we'd had the Hurricanes the British promised!"

"Peacock was right, wasn't he?"

"Oh, he was absolutely right. Bastard French! Bastard British! Sorry," Staś said, crestfallen. Gus thought he looked utterly worn out. "The real bastards are the Nazis, Gus. They bombed civilian targets, churches, schools, hospitals. Nothing was spared. They strafed civilians on the ground. They machine-gunned women and girls out picking potatoes. They even targeted a civilian funeral party in one of Warsaw's cemeteries. Can you believe it? I saw a flight of Stukas diving on small towns, the sirens on their undercarriages screaming, setting buildings and people alight. Of course, I attacked them, but there were too many. I couldn't drive them off."

The port was finished. "Shall I open another?" asked Gus.

"Yes please."

As Gus opened the bottle, his cousin carried on with his tale of woe.

"My friend, Jan Grudziński bailed out after his P-11 was hit. He was floating down to earth, then I saw a Bf-110 open fire on him. Jan was killed instantly; he was completely defenceless. I chased the bastard and got in close, very close, and I hit him. But he got away from me — he pulled to starboard. I wasn't expecting that, and once he had the edge on me his plane was too quick.

"One day I was hit by a Bf-110. It riddled my P-11 with bullets and shot the control stick from my hand. My plane went into a nosedive and I tried to bail out, but the G-force pinned me into the cockpit. I prayed, Gus. I prayed, like the most devout of us. Can you believe it? The P-11 rolled, and I managed to drop free so low that the chute barely had time to open. As it did, that bastard of a Nazi pilot came in and had another blast at me. It was from the same group that killed Grudziński. I was only saved by a Polish fighter that swooped down at top speed and made him flee. I'll never forget those Bf-110s: the nose and the two engine cowlings were painted bright yellow and beneath the nose were shark's teeth, picked out in white on red."

"Bloody hell, Staś!"

"And now the Reds are in Poland too. It's a mess. A disaster."

Staś told his cousin everything he had learned about fighting the Luftwaffe. He explained how the Messerschmitt Bf-109 was faster and much more manoeuvrable than the 110, but the latter packed a much more powerful punch. The Stuka was no use in a dogfight. The German bombers were fast and could out-pace a P-11, but would be no match for a Spitfire, and the Heinkel He-111 was especially vulnerable to attack from behind. Gus, for his part, committed the knowledge to memory in the hope it would be of use to him one day.

"How did you get out of Poland?"

"It was confused. Bloody awful. Tunio Nowacki received orders to take fifty cadets to Romania, where British fighters were supposed to be waiting for them. That's the last I saw of Tunio. My Kościuszko Squadron was moved from Warsaw to Lublin. I took my P-11 and flew the six hundred kilometres from Lublin to Suczawa in Romania. Crossing that border was a horrible moment for us, Gus. I had tears in my eyes. I still don't know if I will ever return. I don't know if I'll see my parents again."

"Of course you'll see them again. This war is going to end soon, I'm sure of it," said Gus, feigning optimism.

"I left the P-11 in Suczawa and stowed away on a train going to Bucharest. There I went to the British Embassy. I had no papers to prove I was a pilot, but speaking English helped. I told them my uncle had been a diplomat in Warsaw but was now ill and that I wanted to get to England. They got me out very quickly, thank God. Then I went to the Polish Embassy in London — they're organising things."

"But all the other Poles — they can't have got out that way, can they?"

"Many did. Others went different ways."

Staś explained that there was no meaningful resistance left in the Polish forces. For a Polish flyer who wished to carry on the fight, the only thing to do was to flee Poland and get to Romania and the British fighters they'd been promised. Tens of thousands of Polish soldiers, air force ground crew and some pilots joined the refugees and crossed the border into Romania.

"Tunio wrote to me about it. He told me they'd turned into a dirty, unshaven lot, their uniforms torn and tattered. All they wanted to do was continue the fight. At the border, Tunio and the Poles were greeted with smiles and back-slaps by Romanian soldiers. It was a sham. He found out later that the Romanian Government had declared itself neutral in the war and wouldn't accept the British and French shipments of planes. There were no fighters waiting for them, Gus. Nothing. Instead, Tunio and the cadets were rounded up and interned. They slept on lousy mats in hovels where they swatted away malaria-infested mosquitoes."

"Poland has been badly let down," said Gus.

"After that, Tunio and hundreds more Polish troops were marched to another camp. He said a middle-aged man in a tatty military uniform came up to him and thrust a small parcel into his hands. It was Romanian money for him and his men — they were to use the cash to bribe guards and soldiers, while staying well away from the police. Orders were to split up into small groups, escape, and make their way to Bucharest any way they could. Once there, they were to hand themselves over to the British or French Embassy."

"So, there was some organisation. There was a plan, of sorts," said Gus.

"It was something."

"And Tunio wrote to you with all of this?"

"Yes, he did. He wrote that he distributed the papers and money and told the cadets to split up and drift off the march as best they could. If they couldn't get away before the next camp, they were to bribe the guards. After all, the guards are soldiers too, and they dislike the Germans almost as much as we do. The cadets were then to make their way to Bucharest and the embassies. Tunio and some of the others got clear of the column at a toilet break, made their way to a railway station, laid low to elude the guards then boarded a passenger express bound for Bucharest just as it was departing. In

Bucharest, they were given more money and directed to a 'safe' hotel by the Polish military attaché's office. They were told Romania was alive with Gestapo on the hunt for Polish pilots and troops. They had to get rid of anything that identified them as Polish military. An official gave them civilian clothes and false identity papers."

"It seems the Poles had an organised, impressive outfit out there. That's something."

"I suppose so," agreed Staś. "In the basement of the military attaché's office, Tunio found embassy officials busy forging passports and visas. They had a courier system working; many young women were putting themselves at risk taking money, clothing and forged papers to the camps. An official gave the men their new identities, then Tunio asked for orders. He was told to make his way due east to the Black Sea ports; Balcic and Constanza were best. That was how many of them got away. A week later, Tunio and three cadets were amongst the seven hundred and fifty Poles packed on board a reeking old Greek freighter. He wrote to me on board, addressed the letter care of the Polish Embassy in London and posted it once the boat had landed in France."

"He knew you'd made it."

"Tunio hoped I'd made it. We cling onto hope, Gus. It's the only thing we have left."

"What will you do now, Staś?" asked Gus.

"Stay here a few days, if I may…"

"Of course."

"I want to go to the Polish Embassy and try to find out about my parents. Then I'll go to France. There are some Polish pilots and ground crew posted to Luxeuil — it's in the East, near the German border. I want to find them and fight with them. Maybe Tunio will get there too, I don't know. If

I'm honest, Gus, I'd rather fight the Nazis in a Spitfire than a Morane-Saulnier, but really, I don't care. What about you?"

"Good news! I've been accepted into the Royal Auxiliary Air Force. I have a temporary commission as a pilot officer. I start my training in October."

"Training?"

"I know. They have their ways."

"It's great news anyway, Gus. We'll fight the Nazi bastards together!"

PART TWO: PHONEY WAR TO DUNKIRK

CHAPTER 5

September 1939

The Air Force insisted that even recruits like Gus, with 'on paper' qualifications and experience, began by proving their capabilities in practice. He was posted to No. 4 Elementary Flying Training School in Brough, an old flying club belonging to the Blackburn Aircraft Company. Flying began with a couple of days of accompanied flights in a Tiger Moth. If the recruits got through that, they moved on to solo flying. If they failed, they had to start from scratch.

Gus's training had gone well, apart from a few heavy landings. He was ready to go solo. It was time to show them what he could do. Gus took the elderly biplane up to three thousand feet and executed the statutory manoeuvres. Coming in to land, he was keen to follow his old instructor Larry Hislop's advice. *Keep calm. Don't be so hasty, especially on landing approaches.* Yes, he was determined to convince the RAF that he was a good pilot.

Gus held the Moth at sixty miles per hour with a little bit of power. Slightly sideslipping now and again to track his centreline, he stuck his head out into the breeze to see where he was heading. *Stay in balance. She's a little high. Sideslip to correct.* The first landing was perfect.

Instead of bringing the Tiger Moth to a halt, Gus opened the throttle and zoomed into the blue. At one thousand feet, he looped-the-loop, blood rushing to his head. Then he approached the grass strip once more, flying downwind and holding the Moth in a shallow dive to increase his speed.

Flying over the Nissen huts, Gus pulled back on the stick, bringing the plane up into a steep climb. When the biplane's nose position was above the horizon, Gus relaxed the elevator input, allowing the Moth to lose airspeed as it climbed. He applied slight rudder to increase the bank and when he sensed the Moth's airspeed slow enough, he applied hard rudder with the pedals.

The Tiger Moth went into a sweeping flat-turn. As if pivoting on its lower wingtips, the upper wings cartwheeled over the top. As soon as the Moth reached a nose-down bank and altitude, Gus released rudder and dived, pulling back on the stick to level the Moth out at the original altitude and into the wind. Once again, he executed a perfect landing on the Brough strip.

Trainees and ground crews surrounded the biplane as Gus got himself out. All bar one were clapping and cheering.

"I've never seen anything like it!" exclaimed Flight Sergeant Jago.

Gus had executed a perfect wingover that he doubted his instructors could manage. "Very few aircraft can accomplish it," he said. "It needs a plane with a low stalling speed. The Moth's ideal. It's not so hard to do, actually. Just requires a lot of rudder."

"Aye, that. And a bloody good pilot with the 'feel' and nerve to come within a couple of miles an hour of the stall," replied Jago. "Well done, sir!"

The training officer, Flight Lieutenant Percy Weatherdon, had a different opinion. Taking Gus aside, he said, quietly but with venom, "You bloody cowboy, Beaumont! Do that again and I'll have you busted!"

Gus stopped himself from attempting to defend his position. He knew there was no point. "Yes, sir," he said through gritted teeth.

Weatherdon's anger didn't hinder Gus's progress, and soon after being signed off on basics he moved onto advanced training.

Seventeen of them, all pilot officers, sat in a classroom.

"You'll be flying the Miles Master," said the commanding officer of their new training establishment, "a low-winged monoplane with a powerful engine. Anyone flown monoplanes before?"

Three hands went up, including Gus's.

"You first," said the CO, "and please tell everyone who you are."

"Stewart Poore. Poorly to my friends. I flew Polikarpov I-16s in Spain, sir. They're Russian planes — fighters. Moscas, the Republicans nicknamed them. Though the Fascists called them Ratas."

"And are they any good?"

"I'll say. Fast, manoeuvrable and armed with two MGs and a couple of 20mm cannon. The Polikarpovs dominated the enemy Heinkel and Arado biplanes the Nationalists were using. They were pretty much unchallenged until the arrival of the Bf-109s."

"And you?" The CO was looking at Gus.

"Oh, I had a go in a Polish fighter before the war, sir."

"You 'had a go'? You make it sound like riding a bike."

"It was, erm, unofficial."

"And you are?"

"Gus Beaumont. Bouncer, sir."

"And yourself?" asked the CO, looking at the third trainee.

"Robert 'Paddy' O'Brian, sir. I was co-pilot of a De Havilland Comet. London to Lisbon route, sir."

Every pair of eyes in the room settled on O'Brian, even the CO looked impressed. "Well," he said, "perhaps you can enlighten us about that, sometime."

After their first flights in the Miles Masters, the trainees chatted in the mess.

"A De Havilland Comet?" said Stewart, looking at Robert. "You must tell us what that was like, Paddy."

"Fast," said Robert. "Incredibly fast. But it was such a bloody boring flight. I'd much prefer to be up in a Spitfire or a Hurricane. I really hope I get selected for single-engine fighters."

"Don't we all?" said Stewart.

"You volunteered in the Civil War, Poorly?" Gus asked.

"No. I was well paid, actually." Stewart laughed. "I got a thousand US dollars a month and another thousand for every aircraft I shot down. I bagged five, but the buggers only paid me for three."

"Many did volunteer," said Robert.

"Not in the air force. On the ground, yes. Bloody fools."

"Why do you say that?" asked Gus.

"Because they were massacred!"

"Can I ask you a serious question, Poorly?"

"Go ahead."

"Would you have fought for the others? The Fascists? If they'd have paid you more, I mean?"

Stewart looked at his beer as he considered Gus's question. "No," he said eventually. "I've got my bloody principles!"

Training successfully completed, the young airmen were eventually posted to their first squadrons. Gus was on his way to Southampton. He got off the train at Euston, and, with plenty of time to spare, instead of taking the underground to Victoria, he decided to take a stroll across the city. The streets were littered with sandbags and slit trenches. Everyone he saw was carrying a canvas bag, which he knew contained their gasmasks. He sauntered through Piccadilly towards Soho. Turning a corner onto Wardour Street, he almost collided with a young woman walking towards him.

"Well, I say!" she said. "That uniform really suits you. It is you, isn't it? Gus? Gus Beaumont?"

"Eunice Hesketh! Bloody hell!" Gus stared for a moment. A few years previously, Eunice had been his girlfriend. They hadn't parted on the best of terms, but he found he was still glad to see her. "What are you doing here?" he asked.

"Don't be silly — I live here, Gus," Eunice said with a smile. "Or should I call you Officer Beaumont? What rank are you? I've no idea what that braid means." She gently touched the single braid on his sleeve.

"Oh, I'm a Pilot Officer. Lowest of the low, actually. I say, do you fancy a spot of lunch, Eunice?" he asked. "It's that sort of time, isn't it?"

"No. It's almost teatime, actually. We could go somewhere for a cuppa. Might get some cake if we're lucky."

They sat at a small table in a tearoom off Greek Street known for playing American swing and big band music. One or two couples danced slowly around a small space reserved for dancing. They ordered a pot of tea and some scones. Gus was ravenous.

"Sorry," he said as he ate. "I skipped lunch today. I've been a bit busy."

"Doing what?"

"I've been training up north, but I'm on the move. I've just been posted to a unit in…"

"That's nice. Maybe we could see a bit more of each other again…"

Gus looked at Eunice. He still found her bright, flashing eyes and broad smile very attractive, but…

"Don't stare," she said.

"Look, Eunice, I'm not sure I can go through anything like that again."

"I'm sorry. It was just that … it wasn't a good time for me."

"And Murray Parkinson? Was it a good time for him?"

"Oh, don't be silly. Nothing happened between Murray and me. I'd decided things might be getting too serious with you and, as I say, it wasn't a good time. So, I picked him up at a party and hung out with him for a while, mostly to make sure you moved on."

"I didn't," he said.

"I can see that. Shall we dance?"

"I thought I was supposed to ask you?"

"Go on then."

Gus stood. "Would you care to dance?" he asked, theatrically.

Eunice accepted and they made their way onto the dance floor.

"What did you do with yourself after dropping out of university?" Gus asked as they danced a foxtrot.

"Nothing much. Took up fashion modelling."

"Fashion modelling?"

"Yes. And don't you look at me like that!"

The music stopped and they went back to their table.

Eunice took a sip of tea. "There's nothing wrong with modelling, is there?" she asked.

"No. No, of course not. It's just that you're so intelligent, Eunice — I thought…"

"That it's beneath me?"

"No. Of course not. So, is that all you do now?" As he asked, Gus hoped he hadn't emphasised the word *all*.

"Yes, it is. I was working this morning, as it happens. But look, Gus, if you don't approve…"

"Stop," Gus said. "Stop. Let's not argue. It doesn't matter. Tell me about it, will you?" He looked at Eunice's face. She was hiding something, he was sure of it.

"The first time I entered a photography studio, Henry Pillinger, the director, told me I have a body that was made to display clothes and that no one would notice me. He told me that everything hung perfectly on my flawless figure. Those were his words. I wondered if it was Henry's idea of flattery. Nobody would notice me, Eunice Hesketh, the Oxford-educated woman within the clothes. No, they wouldn't notice me at all. For one of the shoots, Henry got me to pick up a cigarette and light it. 'Take a drag and blow smoke through those delicious lips of yours,' he said. I hated it, Gus. I still bloody hate it."

"Then why do it?"

Eunice smiled at him. "I told Henry I don't like the taste of cigarettes. 'Oh, do just get on with it, Eunice dear. Be professional,' he said. 'Professional?' I shouted at him. 'You're going to pay me, are you?' But he just carried on telling me to take it seriously. So I pouted and posed and pulled my hair forward, then pushed it back again, while Henry took photographs of me. There were hundreds of bloody photographs. I looked past the camera rather than at it. That's what models do."

She took a sip of tea and then carried on. "We took a break, then Henry said he wanted to photograph me in tweeds. The suit was hanging on a cane manikin. It was various shades of brown and dark green, and it was heavy, coarse and itchy. I thought it was grotesque, Gus. After another hour, the inevitable question came up. 'Now, Eunice, can I persuade you to do a topless for me? Or even just a swimsuit session?' Henry asked. 'No!' I shouted. But he never gives up."

"Have you?" asked Gus.

"Done a topless session?"

He blushed, but Eunice didn't.

"Just once. Henry showed no interest at all in my body. That was a relief, at least. I think he probably prefers men. Most of the shots were of my back, and when I faced the camera, Henry had me hold a handbag in front of my breasts. All I remember was being cold. To this day, I have absolutely no idea where the bloody pictures ended up. Now, I hate the idea. I hate Henry at times. If I'm perfectly honest, Gus, I hate all of it."

He looked uncomfortable.

"Well, you did bloody ask," she said. "Anyway, what about you?"

"I tried to tell you — I'm moving to France. I've been posted to an army liaison squadron."

"Oh my God, Gus."

"I'm bloody disappointed, actually. I wanted to go to a fighter squadron."

She was staring at him, a look of concern in her eyes.

"It's going to be all right, Eunice. You needn't worry. It's not what I wanted, to be honest. I fancied a Hurricane or Spitfire squadron, but they told me my eyesight isn't quite up to the mark. Funny, because I've never noticed anything wrong with my eyes. But don't worry. Nothing's happening over there. I wish it would, to be honest. This blasted Phoney War!"

CHAPTER 6

May 1940

Banking slowly to port, the high-winged Westland Lysander with its large, Perspex cockpit canopy provided Gus with an uninterrupted view over the vast French countryside. He was out on one of his daily reconnaissance sorties, and so far everything looked peaceful. His observer, Flight Sergeant Bernard Chester, was close by.

Gus took in a pretty hamlet dominated by two large white houses with red tiled roofs. A farmer strolled towards a small herd of cattle grazing undisturbed in a field to the left. A flock of blackbirds suddenly rose from the woodland directly below and, as if with a single mind, turned to their right and flew away into the distance. In the morning light, Gus thought the scene was as pleasant as anything this troubled land had to offer. It was also tediously dull, as usual.

"Nothing there, Skipper," Chester announced through the RT.

"Right-oh! We'll get back for a brew then, shall we?"

Gus Beaumont trusted Bernard Chester not to miss a thing. Chester was a veteran RAF reservist, had been in France since October last year and had eight months' experience in his job. Gus suspected they had been paired purposely. Chester was the steady, older hand — an ideal counter to Gus, whose youthful eagerness occasionally made him seem hot-headed.

The Lysander turned and headed towards base. There was nothing to report. The newspapers back in London had dubbed the troops' recent period of inactivity 'The Phoney War', and Gus was sick of it.

"Something's wrong, Skipper," announced Chester over the RT. "Something's disturbed the birds, and I think I can see movement in those trees behind us. Go back and make another pass, will you?"

"If you think so, Flight."

Gus shifted the Lysander into a 180 degree turn to starboard and flew slowly back towards the trees, banking again as the aeroplane reached the edge of the woodland. As he did so, he spotted motorcycle combinations emerging from the cover of the trees. *Germans.* They were accelerating and fanning out as they moved quickly towards the hamlet.

"Blimey!" said Chester. "Jerry's on the move!"

Instinctively, Gus turned to pursue the motorbikes.

"What are you up to, Skipper?" asked Chester, nervously.

Gus ignored the older airman's question. He put the Lysander into a dive and swooped down onto the Germans from the rear. He slowed even more to give himself maximum firing time. *Closer. Closer.* Then a three-second burst of fire from the Browning machine guns housed in the Lysander's wheel fairings showered on the motorbikes. One of the combinations swerved as its driver was hit, crashing into a second.

In the time it took to circle again Gus saw more, heavier vehicles break cover. He counted fifteen tanks and some half-tracks.

"Enemy armour! Lots of it and moving westwards fast," he said.

"Get on the blower, Flight. Let HQ know what's going on down there."

"Roger, wilco Skipper."

As he was radioing base, Flight Sergeant Chester spotted what they both feared. "Bandits, three o'clock!" he shouted down the RT. "Bf-109s, two of them, and they're closing fast!"

Gus cursed his aircraft. With its high, ungainly wings, struts, fixed under-carriage and swollen engine cowling, the Westland Lysander was not built to fly at high speed. Easy to fly and very forgiving to the pilot, these aircraft had been designed to be slow. *No match for a Messerschmitt 109 with a dive speed of 350 mph*, he thought, *and I've got two of them to deal with.*

"Have you made that radio call?"

As the flight sergeant began to speak, the leading 109 opened fire and bullets spat into the Lysander's cockpit, the shattered Perspex striking Gus.

As the first 109 sped by, Gus intuitively knew that the pilot of the second one, the wingman, would by now have the Lysander in his sights.

Think, think! The Lysander might be slow, but it was almost impossible to stall. Gus throttled back and lifted the Lysander's nose. The aeroplane responded by losing speed at an alarming rate. The Messerschmitt went hurtling by, raining machine-gun fire into empty space.

As the 109 flew harmlessly overhead, Gus selected a course that would take him and Chester back to base, and to his relief the two German pilots didn't bother them again. As he landed his bullet-holed Lysander and worried about the condition of his flight sergeant, Gus had just one thought in his head. *The Phoney War is over.* Jumping out of his aeroplane, Gus waved frantically for an ambulance, then dashed over to Flight Lieutenant Johnny Turpin — the squadron leader's adjutant — to make his report. An hour or so later Johnny Turpin reappeared, "Grindlethorpe wants to see you, Bouncer," he said. "You'd better come quickly."

Gus followed Johnny to Squadron Leader Titus Grindlethorpe's office. As he closed the door behind him, he saluted and prepared to face his ire.

"What the bloody hell were you doing?" roared Grindlethorpe. "Did you think trying to shoot up a bloody panzer regiment with a Lysander was going to get you a medal? Did you think it would help at all?"

"I'm sorry, sir," said Gus. "It seemed to be the right thing to do at the time."

"It was very much the wrong thing to do, Beaumont."

"Yes, sir," he said.

"Flight Sergeant Chester is a damned good NCO, and he's been shot down because of you. You are very lucky indeed that he managed to radio through observations before he went down. You could have lost the bloody aircraft. What have you got to say for yourself?"

"Sorry, sir," said Gus.

"I will be watching you, Beaumont," said Grindlethorpe darkly. "Don't you dare try anything like that again. Dismissed!"

Soon after the disastrous sortie, German forces poured over France and the squadron moved back to England. Gus was devastated when he later found out that Chester had died on the boat that had evacuated him. He would forever hold himself responsible.

Two weeks after the squadron had arrived in England and settled into its new base at RAF Sawbridgeworth in Hertfordshire, Squadron Leader Grindlethorpe summoned Gus to his office.

A half-length mirror was mounted on the back of the door of Gus's tiny room in the officers' mess. As he stood before it, he wiped away specks of dust from the corner of the glass. He wore a freshly ironed shirt and ensured his necktie had the best Windsor knot that he could manage. Since Grindlethorpe was known to be a stickler for appearance, Gus brushed his tunic thoroughly before putting it on and buttoning it up. He took a deep breath, grabbed his side-hat and walked out of the door.

He was aware of the glances from his comrades, but nobody said a word as he marched over to the headquarters office. Johnny Turpin was there to meet him.

"Good luck, Bouncer," he said with a wry smile. "You're going to need it. Grindlethorpe is in a stinker of a mood this morning."

"Thanks," said Gus.

"You're welcome." Johnny opened the door into the squadron leader's office. "Pilot Officer Beaumont for you, sir."

Gus walked smartly in, stood to attention in front of Grindlethorpe and saluted, always best whenever in doubt. Johnny closed the office door behind him.

"Stand at ease, Pilot Officer."

Gus did so.

"I haven't forgotten your conduct in France, Beaumont. I have spoken to my superiors. If it wasn't for the fact that England needs every pilot the RAF has, I'd have you discharged," said Grindlethorpe. "As it is, I'll have to keep you. But I've got a special job for you — a rather dangerous one. You're going back to bloody France. Report to Flight Lieutenant Turpin for instructions. Dismissed!"

Gus straightened himself and saluted. He turned towards the door and, as he did so, he thought he heard Grindlethorpe muttering something about him "not returning."

"Here are your orders," said Johnny, handing him a sheet of paper with typed instructions on it. "Some of our pongos are stuck in Calais, and you're to fly out supplies for them. Easy!"

"Thanks," said Gus. "Grindlethorpe hopes I'm not going to return from this job, doesn't he?"

"Look, Bouncer, none of us think you did much wrong. All the mess insist they would have done the same in the heat of the moment. Chester copping it was just bad luck. Those 109s would have jumped you anyhow, and you did well to get back at all."

"Thanks, Johnny. Much appreciated!"

"Anyway, at least we have something to do now the Germans have attacked," said Johnny. "Good luck. You'll come back in one piece — nothing to worry about."

CHAPTER 7

One good thing about Lizzies, thought Gus as he flew at low level across the sea, *is they don't need much runway to land on.* He soon found the airfield and brought the Lysander down with only the hint of a bump, much to the relief of Thomas Morton, the young air-gunner in the back. Gus parked the Lysander then felt down by his left hand for the tail trim wheel, which was beside the throttle. He moved the wheel until it was fully forward, ready for take-off. He'd been taught that it was always best to do this when you landed.

"You stay put and keep a lookout, Morton," he ordered, "and if you see the Luftwaffe, give me a wave."

Gus climbed down from the cockpit. He noticed a group of soldiers standing by a searchlight and anti-aircraft gun on the outer edge of the runway. He ran across the strip towards them.

"Who's in charge here?" asked Gus.

The soldiers turned and examined him, deciding if Gus was senior enough to warrant smart attention. One of them decided he wasn't. "Me. I'm in charge here," said the sullen NCO.

"I mean your officer. Where is he, corporal?"

The soldier waved in the direction of a brick shed a hundred yards away. "He's over there, in the guardroom."

"In the guardroom, *sir*!" bawled Gus. "And if you don't salute me when addressing me, I'll see to it that you're busted back to private." He stared into the soldier's eyes.

"You'll find the lieutenant in the guardroom, sir!" the soldier added, saluting smartly.

Gus returned the salute, ran over and flung open the guardroom door. He was confronted by a fresh-faced second lieutenant sitting at a small desk, looking at a map. The army officer looked up, and Gus recognised Duncan Farquhar, an old friend from his university days.

"Gus Beaumont," said Duncan, clearly surprised. "Last time I saw you, you were properly pissed-up in the Turf Tavern. What on earth are you doing here, old boy?"

"Bloody hell, Duncan," said Gus. "I could ask the same of you. I thought you were with the Ox and Bucks territorials. What are you doing here?"

"I transferred my commission to the Royal Engineers in '38. I've been here since February. I'm with the 1st Searchlight Regiment, Royal Artillery," Duncan replied proudly.

"You're in charge of that lot by the light, then?"

"Certainly am. A fine group of men."

"A surly bunch, I'd say. Especially that corporal."

"Oh, you must mean Lance Bombardier Cooper? Yes, he can be. Good soldier, mind. It's not his fault he's bad-tempered. They can all see it's going badly, and naturally enough they blame their officers."

"Aren't the French to blame?"

"They're certainly not holding up too well, but I'm sorry to say we're just as bad. Wish I hadn't been sent here if I'm honest, Gus. Complete bleeding cock-up!"

"Really?"

"Yes, really! Complete breakdown of military administration. Do you know, an armoured unit arrived here a few days ago, but their tanks were still in Southampton. When they eventually turned up the engines had been taken apart and waterproofed for a sea voyage. Regulations, apparently. Some motorised reconnaissance boys arrived without their motorbikes and machine guns. They're armed with bloody revolvers — can you imagine it? Do you know the heaviest weapon my searchlight troop is armed with?"

"No idea," said Gus.

"A Boys anti-tank rifle. Yes. Here we are with a panzer division surrounding Calais, and all my lads have is a single Boys anti-tank rifle to hold them off! Anyway, enough of that. I see you've got your wings."

"Yes. Thought I might make it to a Spitfire squadron, but the RAF decided my eyesight isn't quite up to scratch."

"Rotten luck. What can I do for you, anyway?"

"I've got a package of spare parts, and I need to get them to 229 Anti-Tank Battery. Know where they are?"

Duncan looked at the map. "Yes, they're manning one of the roadblocks. Here." He pointed to a spot on the map. "I'll see to it for you, if you like. I'll take it myself straight away; it'll only take half an hour. I want to make a patrol anyway. See what's what with my own eyes."

"Righto. I'll come along, if that's all right with you?"

"Look," said Duncan, drawing Gus's attention to the map. "Calais is completely surrounded by the Boche. Come along if you want to, but you may not get out. If I were you, I'd get back in that Tin Lizzie of yours and fly off to Blighty. You can do some good there. I'll make sure your cargo gets to 229 Battery."

It was only then that Gus realised the severity of the situation. Duncan was right: it was Gus's duty to get himself and Morton home and back out on another mission as soon as possible.

Gus nodded his agreement. "I'll be off then," he said. "Good luck, Duncan!"

The two shook hands and saluted.

"We're doomed here," said Duncan, looking depressed. "The lucky ones will be those captured. If I'm taken alive, I swear that I'll bloody well do everything I can to escape, you mark my words!"

There was a strong easterly wind blowing over the northern French coast that afternoon. Gus felt again for the Lysander's tail trim wheel and checked its position. *Get that wrong,* he reminded himself, *and you crash.* There was no way of countering a badly trimmed tailplane once the Lizzie was powering along a take-off runway.

The wheel was ready for take-off. Gus taxied to the leeward end of the strip. With the brakes on hard, he pushed forward on the throttle lever with his left hand to open up the powerful Bristol Mercury engine of the Lysander. When it was almost up to maximum prop speed, he let off the brakes. The Lysander was airborne within yards and heading due east, into the wind.

It was then that Gus saw the Bf-110.

It came out of the sun in a textbook attack. Gus glanced towards the German aircraft as it closed in on him, noticing the evil-looking shark's teeth painted onto the yellow nose of the aircraft. The RAF manual stated that the Bf-110's maximum speed was over 250 knots, but he knew it wouldn't need to go that fast to get the Lizzie in range. There was no way he could outpace it. He had only seconds before the machine guns housed in its nose, firing at 1,200 rounds per minute, would release a torrent of bullets into the Lizzie. As if that wasn't enough, the 110 also had two 20mm cannon that would rip his aeroplane apart.

Instinctively, he rolled the Lizzie to starboard to take it towards rather than away from the 110 and pointed her downwards. He saw flashes from the nose of the Messerschmitt, felt the impact of bullets tearing into the

Lysander, and saw waterlogged ground very close in front of him. Levelling the Lizzie and slowing her as much as he could, Gus called out on the intercom, "Brace, brace, prepare to pancake!" He and Morton braced themselves, then felt the impact of a crash landing. The ground was soft, and the wheels of the Lizzie's fixed undercarriage dug in, upending the plane.

Gus watched the Bf-110 with the shark's teeth take a course towards the French coast. Its job was done.

"You all right, Morton?" asked Gus.

He loosened the young airman's necktie and unfastened the top buttons of his tunic.

Morton stirred. "Yes, Skipper, at least I think so."

"Then up you get. We're on foot from now on."

"Where are we heading?"

"Dunkirk," replied Gus. "Come on, we need to move."

He helped Morton out of the Lysander, then quickly returned and grabbed his map from the small case on the port side of the cockpit. He checked that the .38 calibre Enfield revolver was in his pocket. It was.

"Let's get rid of these bloody ties, shall we, Morton?" he said, removing his own tie. "There's no Squadron Leader Grindlethorpe to badger us here."

Morton smiled. "Lucky the petrol didn't go up in flames, Skipper."

"He missed us. Well, sort of."

Gus had quickly worked out what had happened. The Lizzie must have seemed too soft a target. That German pilot, confident of an easy kill, had opened fire too soon. Staś had told him that Polish fighter pilots tried to get as close as possible to their quarries before opening fire. Almost to collision point, his cousin had claimed. Gus felt sure the Nazi pilots would have acted in the same way — closed to around fifty yards, then opened fire. He'd been wrong.

Judging from the damage to the Lysander's rear end, the Bf-110 must have been more than five hundred yards away when it opened fire. What's more, the pilot could have only used the 110's machine guns, for the damage was relatively light and, as Morton had pointed out, he hadn't hit the petrol tank. The result was a crash landing and the loss of a Lysander. He and Morton were shaken, but uninjured.

Gus didn't know for sure where they were. He remembered turning away from the coast when the 110 attacked and landing soon afterwards. He felt confident they were in territory held by the Allies but couldn't be sure. There was gunfire and smoke to the west of them. Calais.

The fields were flooded, but once they found a road, the going wasn't too bad. After half an hour, they came to a road sign. Using the evening sun to orient himself, Gus saw that Oye-Plage was to the west of them and Gravelines to the north. He located their position on the map. "We've got about fourteen miles to walk, Morton," he said. "We won't get that far today. We'll need to find somewhere to stay overnight."

At dusk, the two airmen approached a farm near Loon-Plage. Gus banged on the door. It was answered by an old man, his face bronzed and wrinkled by the sun and his hands as big as snow shovels.

The farmer pointed them to a barn. Later he returned with some bad-tasting coffee and a flask of brandy, which was much more agreeable. Morton slept, but the worry of what tomorrow might bring and the scuttling of rats in the straw kept Gus awake.

The next morning the farmer fetched them some stale bread, cheese, and a bottle of white wine. They thanked him wholeheartedly, ate their breakfast quickly and hit the road again. Soon they reached a roadblock manned by a platoon of French infantrymen. The brooding soldiers let them through, one shouting after them in poor English, "Off you go — run home and leave the fighting to us!"

The sky over Dunkirk was alive with Nazi bombers. The Heinkels, Ju-88s and Dornier 17s of the Luftwaffe were flying almost unopposed, with only the occasional Hurricane or French Air Force Dewoitine fighter there to offer any resistance. As they got closer to the town and the beach, the scream of Stuka dive bombers became overpowering.

Eventually, they happened upon a group of buildings that had been attacked from the air. It had the hallmarks of a small airfield: there were burnt-out aeroplane parts scattered around, potholed earth and badly damaged buildings. A burnt-out flak emplacement was surrounded by the bodies of French soldiers.

Morton picked up a rifle and examined it. "Straightforward bolt-operated mechanism, easy as pie," he said. "Want one, Skipper?"

"Put it down, Morton. It'll be no bloody use against a tank, will it?"

"But it makes me feel better."

"Morton, I said put it down. You'll get us both killed if you start waving it around, or worse, shooting it. If we meet any Germans, you surrender to them, and that's an order. Understood?"

"Yes, sir," said the airman, sullenly.

"Anyway, I've got a better plan. Look over there."

Gus was looking towards the one intact building on the badly damaged base. He pointed. "Look there."

It was a high-winged monoplane, a Morane-Saulnier two-seat trainer.

"We're going to fly home! We're going to fly home and fight another day!" said Morton.

"So long as it's got petrol in it," replied Gus as they ran towards the plane and scrutinised it.

"It's seen better days," said Morton, looking at the faded silver body paint and French Air Force markings, peeling away in places.

"But it's been flown recently. Look at those marks in the grass where she's landed," replied Gus, pointing. He walked up to the Morane-Saulnier and felt one of the cylinders on its radial engine. "Lukewarm. Let's see if she's got any petrol."

"Here we are, Skipper." Morton unscrewed the filler cap on the fuel tank to be greeted by the smell of petrol.

Gus climbed up to peer inside the cockpit.

"Can you fly it?" asked Morton.

"We'll soon find out. Let's turn her into the wind."

The two men pushed and pulled the French plane until it was facing into the wind at the end of a longish, flat strip of grass.

"Use those bricks for chocks," ordered Gus, pointing to some debris as he hauled himself into the front cockpit. Once Morton had positioned the chocks, Gus went on, "Right, you spin that prop. Once the engine catches, wait for my signal then kick the chocks away and jump in quick."

It took Morton three swings on the propeller before the engine caught, belching out a thick cloud of blue smoke as it did so. As Gus jazzed the engine two or three times to warm it up, he hoped to God that the Morane-Saulnier didn't have any tail trim adjuster like the Lizzie, or, if it did, that everything was set ready for take-off.

He gave a thumbs-up signal to Morton, who kicked away the makeshift chocks as instructed and ducked under the wing.

Three steps and he was in the rear cockpit. Gus opened the throttle and away went the Morane-Saulnier, just as some figures emerged from a ruined building and ran at them, shouting and bawling in French.

Gus ignored them. He opened the throttle fully and, with beads of sweat on his brow, sent the plane rattling unsteadily along the grassy strip as he struggled with the unfamiliar controls. He was sick with worry, not knowing the stall speed of the aircraft. Were they going fast enough to get into the air? He thought so; it felt right. He pulled back on the control column and the flimsy aeroplane nosed upwards. They were in the air, easily clearing a small group of trees in a neighbouring field.

"You did it!" shouted Morton, relief in his voice.

Once he had gained sufficient height, Gus could see the countryside. Just a few weeks before this had been beautiful, unspoilt pasture. Now it was pockmarked and afire, devasted by war. He looked for the French coastline and turned directly towards it, planning to leave Calais to port and pick up a course towards the Kent coast once he had passed the burning city.

"Look out for fighters," he warned Morton, though what evading action he might take if any were spotted, Gus did not know.

Thick columns of acrid, black smoke billowed skywards from the beaches around Dunkirk. The smoke wafted into the open cockpits of the Morane-Saulnier, making the airmen retch.

Gus looked down. The beaches were strewn with military vehicles broken and smashed by bombs, and bodies were scattered around them. He spotted what looked like a fishing boat, left high and dry on the beach with a group of British soldiers sitting behind it. Elsewhere, lines of men stretched across the sands and into the sea so that those at the front were up to their chests in water. The sea itself was crammed with vessels of all sizes, some heading to France and others away from France. Some were damaged. In one area the sea was on fire, as fuel had spilled from a sinking ship and had been ignited.

Gus saw a long breakwater that had a large vessel moored against it. As he looked, a Heinkel 111 came along the beach from the north. It seemed to be lining itself up for an attack on this structure. Gus could do nothing as the German bomber came closer and closer then dropped its load of bombs — all of which missed their target.

They were halfway across the English Channel and, they hoped, safe from enemy fighters. The sky was almost empty, the sunshine bright and steady. They'd soon be home.

Suddenly, Gus felt the engine misfire. Then it began stuttering and cut out altogether. He found the French aeroplane easy to handle in a glide, but there was no way it would make it to the English coast. He deliberately drifted the Morane-Saulnier across the bows of the boats heading to England, hoping he'd been spotted by at least one of them.

As the plane lost height and approached the sea, Gus tried to lift its nose with the intention of making a level belly flop of a landing. It didn't work. The port side of the fixed undercarriage hit the water first, spinning the plane over to the left and ditching both him and Morton into the sea.

Gus choked and spluttered, coughing out some of the salt water he swallowed. It tasted of petrol. He saw Morton go under. As he resurfaced, the shock of landing in the cold water combined with the fear of drowning consumed him. He was shaking and struggling for breath but managed to scream, "I can't swim!" as he began thrashing around wildly.

Gus swam towards him, determined not to cause the death of his second crewman within a month. His sodden, woollen uniform was slowing him down badly.

Eventually, he reached Morton but found it impossible to grab hold of him. Twice he tried to seize hold, but Morton's incessant thrashing around in the water prevented him. On the third attempt he whacked Morton in the face with his clenched fist, hurting his hand as he did so, grabbed hold of his collar then desperately hung on to him, struggling frantically to keep them both above water.

As Gus was losing strength and beginning to feel the cold, a lifebuoy landed in front of him. He gratefully reached for it.

One of the boats had altered course when it saw the aeroplane crash into the sea. Now it came alongside the two airmen. Gus helped two seamen get Morton, now shivering uncontrollably, out of the sea using a rope sling. Then, dripping water and coughing, he dragged himself up the net, reaching for the hands offered. Aboard at last, he fell onto the deck. The sailors took charge of Morton, moving him inside the vessel. They gave Gus a blanket and a mug of scalding hot tea. He looked around and noticed the name of the vessel painted on a lifeboat: the *Royal Daffodil.*

CHAPTER 8

Gus couldn't stop shivering and his dripping uniform clung to his skin. A friendly sailor had strapped up his bloodied hand and given him a cigarette and, although he didn't smoke them, he gasped at it, trying to keep the thing alight.

A French officer walked by, and Gus thought he recognised him. The man had an impish face and a neat moustache, and he wore small, round-lensed, narrow-rimmed spectacles.

The officer, who Gus now saw was a captain, noticed him staring.

"Excuse me, sir," Gus began. "Is it Monsieur Bloch? Professor Bloch of the Sorbonne?"

"Why, yes," the officer replied in English. "Have we met?"

"In Oxford two years ago, you gave a seminar on the concept of total history."

"I did indeed, and you were there, Monsieur? Well, what a coincidence!"

Gus introduced himself and the two men shook hands.

"One of the crew told me that this ship is almost new," said Bloch. "It was built just last year and — you'll like this — can you guess what it was built for?"

"Tell me."

"The *Royal Daffodil* was built for making pleasure trips across the Channel from London's Tower Pier. Pleasure trips — just imagine!" Bloch sat himself down beside the shivering Gus. "What happened to you?" he asked.

Gus told him his story. He looked around the boat. It was crammed with battle-weary, exhausted men. Most were British soldiers or airmen. Some were French.

"Look at them, Professor Bloch. We're defeated."

"France is broken," said Bloch. "We probably will be defeated. But your boys are simply dog-tired. With luck — and England will need luck to get more of them off those damned beaches — you can rise again."

Gus smiled wearily. "You say France is broken?"

"There's no plan, no thought of a plan, Monsieur Beaumont. Worse, the old generals are completely broken. Let me tell you, I fought in the first war, and when France was threatened, I decided to fight again. I speak English, as you know, and was posted to General Billotte's First Army Group Staff as liaison with the British Expeditionary Force. I was with HQ, and just before a crucial meeting with the British, I caught Billotte muttering away to himself. 'Against these Nazi tanks we can do nothing,' he stammered. 'I'm going to burst with fatigue.' Billotte thought he was tired, but it was worse than that. He was in a state of complete despair. The other French generals are no better — they're just waiting to be crushed," said Bloch and he gazed out to sea, embarrassed.

"My God," said Gus.

"They've put France to shame. A few days later, news came that General Billotte had been badly injured in a motor accident. I couldn't help but think that was a good thing. He'd be no great loss to us."

"Tell me more, Professor. Tell me exactly what happened."

"I first realised something was wrong two days after the German invasion. I was in the centre of Poix-du-Nord with Maurice Pinault. Maurice is an infantry captain, a reservist, but a real soldier, not an administrator like me. Anyway, we spotted a troop of tanks going the wrong way through the town. The tanks were oddly camouflaged, and I didn't recognise the model. But then, I'm no expert on tanks. What I knew for sure was that those tanks were heading west when they should have been going east, towards the enemy. I thought they must be lost. So I sprinted off to gain the attention of the commander of the leading tank to tell him his mistake — do you follow me?"

"Yes," said Gus. "Carry on."

"As I ran towards the tanks, I heard Maurice shouting after me. He took charge. He knew exactly what to do. He quickly commandeered a car and driver, and in we got. I asked where we were heading. I was shaking. Actually shaking. I just couldn't believe my mistake. Maurice told me we were heading to HQ, because we were being overrun more quickly than the generals realised. I said we should telephone them. 'Don't be stupid,' he said. 'The lines are down!' He was shouting now, urging the driver on. In an hour we reached the small chateau that held Billotte's HQ. It was all but deserted, with just a solitary junior officer looking around himself."

Bloch paused. He looked over to the land beyond Dunkirk. Gus followed his gaze and saw plumes of smoke still rising into the sky.

"He was a lieutenant called Eugene Ramuel. Funny how I remember details like that," said Bloch. "We asked him where General Billotte had gone. Ramuel told us he'd moved the HQ to Douai. Maurice asked why he'd moved the HQ, but Ramuel didn't know. He thought Billotte perhaps wanted to be nearer the British. Then he told us that the general was close to breaking point. They're all the same — desperate old men who don't know what to do."

"So this Ramuel, he saw it too?" enquired Gus.

"Yes," replied Bloch. "Ramuel was out on reconnaissance. He spotted a unit of German motorcycle troops, but his armoured car broke down. He left the others with it and took a horse from a peasant to get back with the report, only to find the HQ empty. Douai was forty kilometres away, and we still had the car. We offered Ramuel a lift, but he didn't want to leave his men. Maurice was severe with him; he said that his men were probably either captured by now, or worse. With a pained look on his face, Ramuel agreed."

A sailor came up to them and offered them cigarettes. Gus shook his head, then looked at Bloch. "Do you want to smoke, Professor?"

"British tobacco? No thanks," said Bloch, then continued with his story. "The road north was crammed, so we moved at a snail's pace. By mid-afternoon, the heat of the sun had warmed the earth and the tarmac so much that we could feel its heat. Then we were attacked by dive-bombers. The shriek of sirens was above and behind us. I looked up. 'Stukas!' I shouted. I'll never forget that screaming noise for as long as I live. I learned afterwards how troops could become broken, completely demoralised just by the noise of Stuka attacks. Once the bombers had flown away, we saw that there was little actual damage — some holes in the road and one truck on fire, a wheel missing from its axle. Eventually, we found the new HQ, which had been set up in a redbrick infant school in the suburbs of Douai. Finally we received orders. Maurice Pinault was sent back to Paris. As for Ramuel, he trudged off to try to find his regiment. I'll never forget the look on his face."

"And you?" asked Gus.

"I was ordered to remain in Douai in charge of a section of signallers. We were ordered to move north, and for the following few days we were consistently withdrawing from the Germans, though never quickly enough. Our quarters were in schools, chateaux, a former convent. Each day, by the roadsides, we saw cemeteries from the Great War. Now we were being beaten by the same old enemy. Only this time, the enemy isn't simply powerful and well organised. They are evil. I tell you that as a man and as a Jew."

"I'm Jewish too, on my mother's side."

"Then you are like me," said Bloch. "I never go to shul, but I'm perfectly aware of what's been going on in Germany since Hitler's Nazis came to power. They are bastards!"

"Bastards," echoed Gus.

Bloch nodded and then continued his story. "As we neared Lens, I saw huge, black slag heaps and, at night, I saw the city of Arras burning. Eventually we came to Steenwerck, where I received our final orders. I was to burn all official papers in my possession and make my way, with my men, to a rendezvous at Bray-Dunes, near Dunkirk. The beaches were mayhem! Chock-a-block with disorderly soldiers. Some may have been searching for their units, I thought, if I gave them the benefit of the doubt. In my opinion, most were seized by some sort of hysteria. They weren't soldiers anymore, just an unruly mob. I tried to get some semblance of order instilled into one group of unarmed French infantrymen, but it was no use. Anyway, my responsibility was to my signallers. By then, all daytime boarding of ships had been stopped, but I was assured by an English naval officer that my section would be put on board a British vessel the next night. He was true to his word, but the ship was bombed and sunk. The following day I made it on board this vessel, the *Royal Daffodil*. And now here I am, talking to you. What a strange meeting place for two kindred spirits!"

"Indeed it is," agreed Gus.

Early next morning the *Royal Daffodil*, rocking gently on a calm sea, came within sight of Dover. Gus was mightily relieved to see the white cliffs, the morning sun bathing them in light. He pointed them out to Bloch.

"What will you do now?" asked Gus.

"I'll head back to France as quickly as possible and report to whatever military command I can find. I'll fight, Monsieur Beaumont. I'll fight these Nazis. And if, as I feel sure it will, France capitulates, I know there will be resistance. I'll join. I will resist the Nazis in whatever way I can. What about you?"

"Well, this will need seeing to," he said, waving his bandaged right hand, "then I'll report to my CO, Squadron Leader Grindlethorpe. I have some explaining to do."

"I sincerely hope we meet again, Monsieur Beaumont. Hopefully in more fortunate circumstances."

"I hope so too, Professor. Do you have a pencil and paper?"

Bloch rummaged in his pocket and found both. "Here!"

Gus scribbled his name, rank and the squadron's address and gave them back to the Frenchman. "If you can, please write to me."

The two men, both volunteers against a tyrannical enemy, one slightly too young to be at war, the other old enough to have been exempt from active service had he so chosen, shook hands. Then they straightened and saluted each other.

CHAPTER 9

While Gus's hand was healing he arranged to meet up with Eunice in London. They met in the same tearoom on Greek Street. The same swing music as before was playing in the background. Eunice wore an elegantly cut summer dress, which Gus thought looked slightly out of place, somewhat continental in style.

"That's a pretty dress, Eunice," he said. "It really suits you."

"Thank you. I bought it in Paris."

"Paris?" he asked, surprised. He thought a look of guilt suddenly passed across her face.

"I've got something to tell you, actually," she said.

A waitress arrived with a tray, on which there was a teapot, a milk jug, a bowl of sugar and two cups and saucers with teaspoons. Eunice took the lid off the teapot and stirred.

"Let it stand for five minutes," said Gus impatiently. "Well, what have you got to tell me?"

"Last year, everyone knew the war was coming, and I wondered what I would do. I'd achieved absolutely nothing in life. Some pictures of me modelling fine clothes in *Harper's Bazaar* and other top-end magazines — well, what was that worth? I wondered whether a war might actually bring me opportunities. In the last war, women had worked in factories, on the land, and as nurses. Not that I really fancied any of that. But surely, war brings change, and change always provides new opportunities — for some. Shall I pour?"

"Not yet. To be frank, I can't see you in a munitions factory, Eunice. Or as a Land Girl. So tell me more."

"Henry — remember I told you about him? Well, after a shoot, he would take me to the Shim Sham Club in Soho. There weren't many girls there. Many of the men wore makeup — glaring lipstick and dark eyeliners. But I noticed that those men very rarely arrived wearing their makeup and most removed it before they left. Everything was very relaxed, though, and I quite liked it there. Sometimes Henry would disappear for an hour or more, leaving me on my own, but I didn't really mind. I loved dancing with the men." She stopped to pour the tea. "Sugar?"

"You can't remember?"

"Oh, yes. One level spoonful. Silly of me."

Gus smiled as Eunice carefully added sugar and stirred his tea. "Do carry on," he said.

"One of the men I met at the Shim Sham was Cedric Burrows. I knew him by reputation as a photographer and designer. He showed a bit of interest in me. Not sexual interest, of course. Nor intellectual. He said I had 'potential' as a model. One afternoon, Cedric took me and Henry to another club — the Gargoyle in Soho. That's where we bumped into an RAF type. He wasn't in uniform, but Cedric introduced him as Alexander Peacock and told me he was in the RAF."

Gus started and spilt tea on his jacket. "Wing Commander Sir Alexander Peacock?" he spluttered.

"Yes, that's right. Do you know him?"

Had she 'bumped into' Peacock? Not likely. It was a set-up. Peacock didn't leave anything to chance.

"I know him, vaguely," he lied. "He was a colleague of my father."

"Well, what a coincidence."

"Such a coincidence. Do tell me more, Eunice."

"Cedric introduced us to Sir Alex and described me as one of Henry's muses. Well, I didn't much like that, but what could I do? Then Sir Alex said he thought he recognised me from some photographs he saw in *Vogue*."

"Eunice, can I ask you something?" said Gus.

"Go ahead."

"Does Sir Alex Peacock strike you as a typical *Vogue* reader?"

"That's interesting. No, he doesn't, and I thought it odd at the time. Peacock didn't look the type to be following fashion."

"He's not. It was a set-up," said Gus.

"What do you mean?"

"I mean Peacock knew of you and wanted to meet you. He set up the meeting at the Gargoyle Club. I doubt he'd ever set foot in the place before."

"Really? But why?"

"Carry on with the story, Eunice."

"Cedric and Henry disappeared, leaving me alone with Sir Alex. He offered to get me a drink, and I asked for a Kir Royale. So he placed an order with the bar boy and asked for a Scotch for himself."

"A Kir Royale? Very French," observed Gus, gazing again at the continental-style dress Eunice was wearing.

"That's exactly what Peacock said. So I told him I'd lived in France — Paris, actually, for a number of years. I rather got into the habit of drinking Kir Royales, I suppose."

"You never told me you'd lived in France," said Gus.

"I had to be circumspect the last time we met — you'll see why when I tell you the full story. But now I know I can trust you. Anyway, I told Peacock I'd lived in Paris —"

"He already knew," said Gus.

"What?"

"That's why he's interested in you, Eunice. You speak French. You've lived in Paris. What did he say?"

"He hardly said a word, now I come to think of it. He let me do most of the talking. I was just about to ask him what he did when Peacock asked me if I'd like to go back to Paris. He must have seen the astonished look on my face, because he immediately assured me that there was nothing illegal or dodgy going on. In fact, I would be going there on behalf of His Majesty's Government. Then he passed me his card and asked me to meet him at the address written on it. I was to go there the following afternoon, at three. Top up, Gus?"

"Yes, please. You don't need to tell me the address. RAF Club, Piccadilly, was it?"

"Why, yes! The next day, as I made my way to the club, I wondered what on earth this mysterious man had in mind for me. I wasn't sure if I should trust him…"

"You mustn't," warned Gus.

"…but he clearly knows Cedric, and he's a Knight of the Realm. Anyway, at the club, Peacock, now in uniform, explained what he had in mind. 'We all know there's going to be a war with Germany soon,' he said. Then he told me there was a chance that France might get knocked out or be occupied by the Germans, and if that happened, our government would need people they could rely on over there. Some would be French, of course, but they might also need British people, people they knew and could trust. Cedric had apparently told Sir Alex all about me, and they thought I might pass as a Frenchwoman. So Sir Alex offered me a month in Paris, all expenses covered."

"What did you say?" asked Gus.

"I was intrigued. I reminded him that my passport is British, but he told me Henry would do some makeup, change my hairstyle, and take new photographs, so we could have a French passport knocked up in no time at all and…"

"Eunice, what did you say?" he interrupted.

"I said yes, of course."

"And so you went to France?"

"Yes."

The music had come to an end. One of the waitresses changed the record and the slow, rhythmic sound of Glenn Miller's 'Moonlight Serenade' began to fill the tearoom.

"I love this tune," said Eunice. "Let's dance?"

Gus nodded and got up. He pompously offered a hand to Eunice. "Might I have the honour of this dance?" he asked.

Eunice laughed and rose elegantly to her feet. "Of course you may, darling," she said. She took Gus's left hand, placing her own on his shoulder. He held her waist and they began to dance. Gus knew that he, as the man, was supposed to lead, but Eunice was a much better dancer, so he let her do the work.

"Tell me about France, Eunice. I'd like to know everything that happened there."

As they danced, Eunice began to relate her story. "I had a fake name, of course — Clarice Delacroix. Rather fetching, don't you think?"

"Yes. It suits you," said Gus, turning at the end of the dance floor.

"I remember after two weeks, standing on the platform of the Gare Saint-Lazare, waiting for a departure to Cherbourg. I was sad to be leaving Paris. The city was so gay and charming, and I was enjoying my time there. True, I didn't have a great deal to do, but Peacock had insisted it was important and would be of great use when the war came. As soon as news of a German breakthrough reached him, he contacted me and told me to get back to England as soon as I could."

"He didn't want a potentially good agent caught up in that chaos," said Gus.

Eunice considered. "Oh? And there was I thinking he was genuinely concerned about my safety." The music finished. "Let's sit a while," she suggested.

"What exactly did you do there, Eunice?"

"I'd reported to my contact, Xavier, as instructed. Xavier, not his real name, obviously, took me to a hotel just around the corner from his small flat on the Rue d'Orsel. The concierge examined my fake identity card with the photo of me staring wide-eyed at the camera, like a rabbit caught in searchlights. Not Henry Pillinger's usual style at all. 'Mademoiselle Delacroix. One month?' he asked. I confirmed and the first test was passed.

"Next day, Xavier showed me around the area and instructed me on where to go if there was an air raid, which was unlikely, he insisted. In the evening, he collected me at reception and took me to a café, where we met some of his acquaintances. He'd already asked me what I drank, so as to appear as if we knew each other. Xavier called to the waiter as he sat down and ordered a Kir Royale for me and a pastis for himself. Then he spoke to a couple already at the table. He introduced me as Clarice, his younger sister, who was staying in Paris for a short while before going south. The man asked me where I was from. I told him Alsace, as I'd been briefed. My cover story, Sir Alex called it. I told them things were 'tense' there. The woman assured me I was welcome in Paris, and that the city was well away from any threat.

"Xavier's friends were correct, so far as I could tell. There was no panic, no mass movement out of Paris. There were few gas masks, and no air-raid sirens. The bustling streets, cafés, restaurants and shops carried on as normal. As the drinks and conversation continued to flow, I knew the second test, to pass myself off as French to ordinary people, would be straightforward. The talk was of the Maginot Line and how it was impregnable — how France had hundreds of thousands of soldier reserves who even now were being mobilised.

"After a few days, the time for my third test arrived. I'd looked around for a small, moderately priced flat to rent. I feigned interest in one of them and the agent took me to view it. 'Good job you're young and fit, mademoiselle,' he said, as he puffed up the two flights of stone stairs, which took us to a locked door on the top landing. He had a horrible, suggestive glint in his eye."

"Not your type at all," said Gus, smiling.

"I told him the flat looked really lovely. It did. The agent told me he could arrange to have the place re-decorated if I wished, then went over to the window to show me the view. I gazed out over the city; I could catch a glimpse of the white-domed Basilica of the Sacré-Cœur if I leaned slightly to my left. *Yes*, I thought, *I could live here.*

"Xavier took me to the agent's office to negotiate the lease. I produced my fake documents and answered his searching, though plainly bureaucratic questions. So, the third test was passed. I could indeed pass as a French national to an official."

"Tell me more about this chap — Xavier."

"I'm not even sure that Xavier's French, but he may be. Or Belgian, or even a Canadian. I just don't know. We never spoke about our backgrounds; we didn't speak much at all, really. Not at first. He was older, and he'd been injured in the Great War, he told me, so he walked with a slight limp. He was tall and good-looking, with a dark skin tone and a moustache.

He wore his black beret at a defiantly jaunty angle and always seemed calm and composed."

"Did you fall in love with him?"

"He was attractive. Somehow, I felt close to him from the start. I suppose it was inevitable, in the situation, that I found him mysterious."

"You did, didn't you?"

"I don't know, Gus, but as I sat in that first-class carriage on the train to Cherbourg, I was deeply sorry to be leaving Paris, France and him. I'd gone there at Peacock's instance to be helpful in the event of a war. War had come and I was being pulled out. Xavier had given me Peacock's instruction to return the evening before. 'What will you do?' I asked him. The army wouldn't take him because of his leg, but he said he'd find a way of fighting the Boche. He looked me in the eye and asked what I'd do. 'I suppose I'll do what Peacock tells me,' I said."

"What do you think he'll ask you to do?" asked Gus.

"Last time I saw him, he said I didn't have to carry on working for him if I didn't want to," said Eunice. "But since I did so well in Paris, he's offered to make me one of his special agents. I said I'd think about it. If I accept, maybe he'll send me back to France."

Gus thought he saw a tear in her eye.

CHAPTER 10

It was the first time Gus had met his cousin since Dunkirk. Over whiskies in the convalescent home, where Gus nursed his wounded hand and Staś a leg injury he'd picked up escaping from France, he told Staś all about seeing the German advance, attacking them and losing Flight Sergeant Bernard Chester. He also told him how he had bumped into Duncan Farquhar in Calais, who they agreed must be in a German POW camp by now, and related what Bloch had told him about the French retreat.

"Good God, Staś," Gus finished, slamming his glass onto the table. "What a bloody balls-up it was!"

"Sounds like it. I'm not surprised, but at least we ended up here. In the same place, eh?"

"Yes, and what a coincidence! So, tell me more about what you got up to in France."

"I remember sitting in the officers' mess at the French air force base in Luxeuil. I was mystified, totally mystified. I looked on as four French pilots tucked into foie gras and a bottle of champagne. They had nothing to celebrate. Earlier that day, I'd been in the air, patrolling with them. We were a flight of Morane-Saulnier 406s — four of us. I spotted a Dornier 17. 'Bandit reconnaissance plane, six o'clock,' I said. Well, I admit, my French is poor. 'Let's get after him!' I shouted."

Staś paused to take a sip of the Scotch Gus had produced. His hands trembled as he reached for the tumbler. "The flight commander's voice crackled into my ears over the RT. 'You can do what you like, Pole,' he said. 'We're going home.'"

"What did you do?" asked Gus.

"I peeled off and pulled the plane into a climb. I wanted to get above and behind the Dornier. Once I had enough altitude, I put the fighter into a steep dive. The engine was screaming, Gus. You should have heard it. Bullets from the one German machine gunner who could get me in his sights were streaming up towards me. I ignored them. They were missing, anyway. I got within two hundred feet of the German plane before opening up with both machine guns and the 20mm cannon. That bloody Dornier erupted into flames!"

"And the French pilots? They went back to base?"

"Yes. After that, all three of them ignored me. But one, a youngster known to the others as l'Andouille, came over to speak to me in the mess."

"What did he have to say?"

"He told me I'd done the right thing. He even thanked me, on behalf of France. He said the French needed to be more aggressive, but he knew that many of his comrades were broken by the last war. Anyway, he said he had good news. More Poles were due to arrive later in the week. They came the following Friday. Ten footsore, tired but rugged-looking Polish pilots. Amongst them was Captain Lech Zynda, who I knew from Dęblin. Am I boring you with all this, Gus?"

"No. Not at all. I'm intrigued. So, what did the new arrivals have to say?"

"I knew Lech of old, of course. He was at the flight academy with me. I was glad to see him. He asked what it was like, and I told him that the French didn't want to fight. 'If I've told them once to hide and camouflage the planes,' I said, 'I've told them a dozen times.' It was no use. Lech said they'd seen the same attitude everywhere. When he arrived in Marseilles, nobody was ready to receive the Poles. They were taken to Istres and shoved into primitive barracks, with smashed windows and straw on the floors to sleep. They even had to pay for hot showers and food. To be honest, he said, they were treated no better than foreign prisoners. One night, the Poles thought they heard gunfire and rushed out, hoping the war had finally come to the French. It was the champagne corks popping! Then Lech took me aside. He told me the call had gone out to Polish pilots to get themselves to England, because the RAF would accept us. He told me Tunio Nowacki was already there. He's flying again. Lech was going to make sure he was on a list and on a ship to England. 'Me too,' I said. Apart from anything else, I'd rather fly a Spitfire than these lousy French fighters."

"Not very good, I take it?" asked Gus.

"Better than a lousy P-11!"

Remembering their flying in Poland, before the war, Gus and his cousin laughed. Then they re-filled their glasses and laughed some more.

"Lech and I borrowed a car with l'Andouille's help and took it for a drive around the Maginot Line fortifications," said Staś. "You can't imagine it. Massive concrete fortresses, dotted with steel cupolas. Cloches, the French called them. Each one had heavy cannons as well as machine guns. The line was about twenty kilometres wide, much wider than either Lech or I had imagined. L'Andouille had all the details. He told us the line stretched for over six hundred kilometres. There were forty-five main forts built at intervals of fifteen kilometres, ninety-seven smaller forts and three hundred and fifty-two casements in between. Lech asked why the fortifications were so wide and deep. L'Andouille explained the line was too big to be manned all of the time. The first few lines, the border posts, outpost and support line, are there to slow down any attack. Meanwhile, he told us, the soldiers will come to occupy the principal line of resistance, which begins ten kilometres behind the border, and is protected by anti-tank obstacles. That's what we were looking at, a great concrete and steel fortress, strewn with cloches and even retractable gun turrets that looked like the turrets from heavy tanks."

"They thought it was impregnable," said Gus as he took a sip of his drink.

"Yes. Thousands of guns. Static and mobile artillery units, anti-tank gunners. And all backed up by infantry. That's why the French flyers wouldn't fight in the air. They didn't think the Germans would attack. Poland could be sacrificed just like Czechoslovakia, they thought, so long as the war didn't actually come to France. But that young fellow, l'Andouille, he saw right through it. He told us he thought the Maginot Line made a frontal attack very difficult for the Nazis, and probably put it out of any equation. So, when they attack us, the Germans will pour through the Low Countries again — just as they did in 1914. If l'Andouille had his way, the Allies would be bombing German factories then and would invade in the spring. He said all we were doing was giving them breathing space to recover from the attack on Poland, bring their troops home, and reinforce the Luftwaffe and the Wehrmacht. He was only a kid, but he was right."

"Yes," said Gus, "he was right. The British Expeditionary Force did nothing in France. The RAF did nothing in France." They recalled how quickly the British forces had been sent to France in 1939 — only to sit around, waiting, then be caught on the hop by the Germans in the summer of 1940.

"And here we are," said Staś.

"Yes. Here we are. Another drink?"

CHAPTER 11

"Let me make sure I have understood the situation correctly, Beaumont," said Squadron Leader Grindlethorpe.

Gus's hand was better, he was back with his squadron and, once again, was being reprimanded by Grindlethorpe. Gus stood at attention before his CO, being cross-examined on what Grindlethorpe perceived to be his misdeeds.

"For the second time within weeks, you disobeyed orders. You failed to deliver the spare parts to the officer commanding 229 Anti-Tank Battery, Royal Artillery."

"Correct, sir. I handed them over to Lieutenant Farquhar, who was going out on patrol and who assured me he would deliver the spares."

"So, you do not know that the spares arrived safely at 229 Anti-Tank Battery?"

"No, sir, I do not."

"You are an absolute disgrace to that uniform, Beaumont. You disobey orders, damage a valuable piece of RAF equipment, putting your crew at risk in so doing…"

"I was shot down, sir! By a bloody Bf-110."

"Be silent, Beaumont! Do not swear at me and don't interrupt me!"

Gus had never seen Grindlethorpe so angry before. *Better keep quiet*, he thought. In any case, there was nothing much to say.

"Then you misappropriate property of the French Government."

Gus felt his jaw drop. "Misappropriate?"

"You steal property belonging to an allied nation, causing damage to it. Finally, you instigate a vessel on vital government duties to alter course to rescue you and your gunner."

There was no use in arguing. Grindlethorpe was intent on throwing the book at him. Gus felt sure he would be dishonourably discharged from the RAF. Well, in that case, he decided, he would enlist as a private soldier in the infantry.

Eventually, Grindlethorpe spoke again. "I will need to seek advice from my superiors on this matter. In the meantime, you are off operations. Grounded! If I could confine you to barracks, I would. Dismissed, Beaumont, and the sooner you are out of my squadron, the better."

Johnny Turpin took one look at Gus's face as he left Squadron Leader Grindlethorpe's office then looked away.

"I'm grounded," said Gus.

"Yes, I know," said Johnny sheepishly. "He's told me to allocate you to supervision of the maintenance of the squadron's vehicles. Sorry, Bouncer old boy."

Gus had nothing to say. Embarrassed, he began to walk away.

"Here," said Johnny, "this might cheer you up. I hope so, anyway." He handed Gus a white envelope.

It was addressed to Gus in neat handwriting and as he walked to the mess, he turned it over and noted the sender's address: The RAF Club, 128 Piccadilly.

Two days later, on the train to London, Gus took the folded letter from the envelope he had stuffed into the breast pocket of his tunic. He carefully reread it, making sure he understood its contents. Wing Commander Sir Alexander Peacock wanted to see him on an urgent matter on Saturday 8th June at the RAF Club. What on earth was this all about?

Once again, he walked from the railway station to Piccadilly. This morning's papers were full of the Dunkirk evacuation news. Surprisingly, it was being told as a story of victory. Gus hadn't seen it that way at the time — he thought it was more like a rout.

Peacock was waiting for him in the same reception room as before, but this time he was alone. *Thank goodness he's in civvies*, thought Gus. *I won't have to salute.*

"Well, well, Gustaw," said Peacock. "Good to see you again. Do sit down. No lunch today — I'm sorry. Must be off for a meeting with the PM. But there's a nice little place just around the corner on Brick Street if you're peckish."

"Can we get onto business, please, Wing Commander, if you don't mind?"

"Now, now! No need to be shirty. You know by now that I won't waste your time. That message you took to Poland has done us very well, you know. More than thirty thousand Polish airmen, soldiers and sailors have made their way here — and you were part of that, Gustaw. I hear your cousin made it to England. And Captain Nowacki."

"Yes. Though neither have been attached to active squadrons yet."

"It will come, it will come."

"Can I ask you a question?" said Gus.

"Of course, go ahead."

"Your friend Squadron Leader Taylor," said Gus, "is he the Pole, Piotr Krawiec?"

"Could be. Yes, could be, but he's not my friend. And yourself, Gustaw, how are you getting along with old Grindles? Sorry, I mean Squadron Leader Grindlethorpe?"

"I assume you know," replied Gus.

"Yes, I know. That's why I wanted to see you. I want to read something to you, if you wouldn't mind. It's the typescript of a letter Grindlethorpe wrote to one of his brothers. Let me read it — it's about you, you see."

Gus nodded. Peacock searched in the pocket of his tunic and brought out a paper. Carefully opening it, he put on his spectacles and began reading.

"It reads as follows:

Dear Julius,

I want to offer you my sincerest congratulations on your recent appointment. Lieutenant-Colonel Julius Grindlethorpe suits you very well and I am sure your battalion of the Buffs (even though they are Territorials) will perform most 'steadily' under your command. Were they still living, our parents would no doubt be cheered to see the success of their three sons. On that note, I have not heard from our brother Augustus for some time, though I know his ship, HMS Hood, is in the Med.

For myself, I'm still with the blasted Lysander reconnaissance squadron I commanded in France, though God knows there isn't a lot for them to do now. What's more, I've some of the most incompetent and contrary articles of flotsam and jetsam anybody has ever seen in one place at the same time. This young Beaumont, for example, another bloody RAAF upstart. He's pranged two Lysanders, killed one crew member and almost drowned another. What's more, he's a bloody Jew and the son of a Polish communist. Anyway, I've grounded him for now and I've asked Sir Alex — you remember Peacock? Good man, one of our type, Julius. Anyway, I've asked Alex to move him on for me.

It's just unacceptable, Julius. Our father didn't fight in the Great War for our armed forces to be infiltrated by people like him! You and I didn't stand side by side with Oswald Mosley in Cable Street to have bloody Reds running things, did we? I wouldn't have people like that in the armed forces any more than I'd have them in the Civil Service or industry. Fifth-columnists, all of them! It's bad enough that Winston has brought in the likes of Bevin into his Cabinet. How can he have a trade unionist serve as Minister of Labour? I just don't understand it.

I have to stop now and there's work to be done, so all the best in the new post and do write soon.

Yours sincerely, your brother Titus."

Peacock took off his glasses and looked at Gus.

"Well?" he asked.

"Where on earth did you get it?" asked Gus.

"I have my ways and means. But what do you make of it?"

"He doesn't like me. Simple."

"No, no, Gustaw. That much is plain. Titus thinks you're a Red. Are you?"

"Of course I'm not a bloody Red."

"Your mother? Was she?"

"Probably. But why ask me? You must know more about her politics than I do. You seem to know everything about most things."

"And what about Grindlethorpe? He doesn't like Reds. Nor Jews, by the sound of it. Do you think he's a Nazi sympathiser?"

"My God, Peacock. He was my CO. How the bloody hell would I know?"

"No need to swear, Gustaw. Anyway, I've got a job for you. A new posting to a better squadron; this one is based in West Malling."

"You're doing what Grindlethorpe asked you to do?"

"He'll think so, and that means he'll continue to trust me and confide in me. But that's incidental. I have a task for you, you see. As I say, new squadron. Maybe a promotion to flying officer if you're lucky. If you do well, that is. What do you think?"

"Tell me more," said Gus.

"We want to know if it's possible to fly from southern England and across into occupied France, at night. To fly in, without being spotted, then fly back again. We think the best way to find out is for a pilot officer — someone like yourself — to try it out for us. And we'd like this pilot officer's opinion on the prospects of a small plane landing there on a grassy strip with not much lighting — one that's flat, of course — and then taking off again. I emphasise, we want an opinion on the latter. I do not wish you to attempt to land."

Gus didn't say a word.

"But Gustaw, this is very, very confidential. No one must know."

Still, Gus remained silent.

"Well, I expect you'll need time to consider. Look, I must be off."

"Are you really going for a meeting with Mr Churchill?" asked Gus.

"Yes, I wouldn't lie to you."

"That was an excellent speech he made the other day," said Gus. "It's lifted everyone!"

"Oh, yes — 'We shall fight on the seas and oceans, we shall fight with growing confidence and growing strength in the air…' I'll tell him you liked it. I wrote part of it, actually."

"You did?"

"And do you know what he said immediately after sitting down in the Commons?"

"No."

"All the members were cheering him, the Labour MPs especially. Winnie said, 'And we'll fight them with the butt ends of broken beer bottles, because that's bloody well all we've got!' What do you think of that? No, don't answer. Let me read another letter." Peacock took out a second handwritten script, replaced his spectacles and began to read:

"Dear Prime Minister,

I write in response to your note of 23rd June 1940 re: friendly foreign armies and resistance following the French armistice.

As you know, a large part of the Polish and Dutch navies are now, effectively, with 'us'. The French Navy, on the other hand, are very likely to be friendly to the Nazis. Even if their crews won't fight, their ships in the Med will be of great use to Hitler and his Italian ally. My advice therefore is that Admiral Somerville's Force H is deployed against the French fleet.

The last consignment of Polish troops was successfully evacuated from St Jean de Luz yesterday. There are now approximately 30,000 Polish soldiers in the UK. Remnants of the Polish Army are being assembled and reorganized in the Glasgow area as the 1st Polish Army Corps under the command of General Marian Kukiel. The key issue going forward is to what extent these troops are to be integrated into the British Army. My strong suggestion is for the government to make an agreement with the Polish leadership to enable all Polish military forces to keep their national identity and military customs under Polish command in conjunction with the British War Office and the British High Command.

The Polish Air Force fought better in Poland than Nazi propaganda would have us believe. Sadly, RAF HQ, especially Fighter Command, refuse to believe this. The Polish airmen served very well in France and those who have made it here, estimated at around 130 pilots with associated ground crew, are ready to fly and to fight. Dowding is committed to relegating experienced fighter pilots to bomber duties, as you know. My recommendation is that we form as many Polish squadrons as numbers allow, with the same arrangement as the Polish Army (above).

The French will be adequately well organised by de Gaulle, and we should trust his judgement as far as possible.

There is an active underground and resistance movement in Poland, and we can expect the same in France, Belgium and Holland. There is, and increasingly will be, resistance. However, resistance in Poland is split between those favourable to the Polish Government-in-exile and others, in the Nazi-occupied area, who are communists.

We can expect similar in France. Some will support de Gaulle, but the Reds will seize an opportunity to further their aims.

Your final question, Prime Minister, was a technical one regarding the possibility of flying agents into and out of France in small numbers. I am in the process of checking this with a practical experiment and will be able to report an answer to you within days.

Yours Aye, Sir Alexander Peacock."

"Yes," said Gus. "I'll do it."

"Good. Then you'll go to Malling to a fighter squadron."

"My eyesight isn't up to it, I'm afraid. It's in my MO report."

"There's nothing wrong with your eyesight, Gustaw. I had that little fallacy inserted into your record."

"You did what?"

"I needed you close to Grindlethorpe. I'll have your medical record adjusted, don't worry. Now, off you go, young man. There's a war to be getting on with."

CHAPTER 12

Gus decided to walk the one and half miles from West Malling railway station to the airfield where his new squadron was based. He pulled down the peak of his cap to keep the sun from his eyes. As he reached the airfield, he paused to wipe the sweat from his brow. He then showed his pass at the guardroom and made his way to squadron HQ.

"We'd have arranged a car to pick you up," said a bright, energetic-looking flight lieutenant. "You only had to ask, you know."

"Sorry, I felt I needed the exercise."

The flight lieutenant offered his hand. "Arthur Holbrook — I'm acting squadron leader. Fellows in the mess call me Keats. And you're Beaumont, I presume. Gustaw. Have a nickname?"

"Bouncer," replied Gus.

Holbrook looked askance.

"Couple of hard landings in the early days."

"Ha! You'll do nicely here, Bouncer, with that sense of humour! C'mon, we'll get you settled and then I'll introduce you to the other chaps."

Holbrook walked at a brisk pace towards a low, redbrick building. He burst through the door and raced up a flight of stairs. Once on the landing, he bounded along the corridor and opened the door to a small room.

"Here you are. All yours."

Gus looked around the room. It was strewn with articles of clothing and books, with a gramophone in one corner. There was a diary laid open on the small desk with a fountain pen beside it. On the same desktop was a framed photograph of a young woman.

"Sorry," said Holbrook. "I'll get it all moved."

"Who was he?"

"Jimmy Prior. Nice young chap. He bought it two days ago when he tried to outrun a 109. He should have lost height and circled, as he was advised to. Bad mistake, that. Where did you say the rest of your gear is, Bouncer?"

"I didn't, but it's on its way. It should be here tomorrow, I think."

"Good."

Holbrook walked him down to the mess where three other officers were sitting around, reading newspapers and smoking.

"Listen up, gentlemen, this is our latest Luftwaffe fodder offering, Pilot Officer Gus Beaumont — AKA Bouncer from now on. Bouncer, this motley crew are…" Holbrook pointed from left to right as, in his own inimitable way, he introduced them:

"These three sturdy fellows from Malling,
Named, Jefferies, Marten and Sparling,
No sport will they take
So for your own sake,
Take their advice: do not go disparaging."

With that, the acting squadron leader hurtled away.

"Don't mind Keats," said Marten. "He's a bit of a whirlwind and joker, but he tends to get things done. You'll just have to get used to his bloody awful limericks, that's all. The others call me Pine, by the way. Where have you come from, Bouncer?"

"From a Lysander squadron."

"Bit of a career change, that," said Jefferies. "What brought you here?"

"Had a bit of bother. The CO wanted me out, so here I am."

"Bother? What sort of bother?"

"I had a pop at some Jerries when I ought to have been steering a course to base."

"Good for you," said Marten. "I'd have done the same myself."

"That's not a sacking offence, surely?" asked Jefferies.

"My observer was shot down."

After a moment of silence, Marten beckoned an orderly. "Get the officer some food, would you, Wonnacott?" Once the orderly had gone off towards the kitchens, Marten turned to Gus. "Sit yourself down, Bouncer. How many hours have you had flying in Defiants?"

"None, I'm afraid."

"Then you'd better get some hours in as soon as possible, certainly before you go up for a sortie. One of us will take you up for a spin after lunch, if you would like to?" offered Jefferies.

"I would, thank you," said Gus.

"I'll take him in G," said Marten. "It needs a test after that fuselage repair. You can sit in the gun turret; I'll talk you through everything. Then you can have a spin yourself. Lunch first, though."

The orderly came over with a plate of steak and kidney pudding, new potatoes, and broad beans.

"Thank you," said Gus, as the food was placed carefully in front of him.

"You are very welcome, sir," said the orderly. "I grew the veg myself out the back."

"This is the mess orderly, Aircraftsman Wonnacott. Good as gold," said Jefferies. "He's a great cook and an even better gardener."

Wonnacott smiled. "I've grown kale and chard to supplement the beans. Onions and carrots need longer in the ground. Parsnips, turnips and broccoli are better off left through a winter. And for your puddings, there's still lots of rhubarb coming, which I can keep on pulling until the first autumn raspberries come into fruit."

"Wonnacott also knows the best herbs to use to flavour the meats and fish," Sparling added. "In the cupboard, alongside the jams he's made from wild fruits, there are jars of crab-apple jelly, which he serves us with pork, and quince jelly, which he serves up with a cheese board. Best of all is his homemade sloe gin, which comes out after dinner. You'll not starve here, Bouncer."

Two hours later, Gus and Marten stood at the side of a Boulton Paul Defiant. Marten was wearing an orthodox flying suit with a parachute; Gus was wearing a Rhino suit.

"I know it's odd," said Marten, "but there's no room in the turret for the gunner to sit wearing a normal chute. So some boffin came up with that."

"Does it work, Pine?" asked Gus.

"I've absolutely no idea, old boy. Getting out of the bloody turret would be hard enough. Once out, it's simply fingers, and everything else, crossed." Marten took a final drag on his cigarette and threw the stub in the general direction of the aeroplane.

"They're that bad?"

"Yes, positively shite. Too bloody slow. It's the weight and drag of the turret that slows the beast down. Not to mention the weight of the bloody gunner! Makes a Daffy a good thirty-five knots slower than a Hurricane."

Gus looked the Defiant over.

"And no forward guns," continued Marten. "You asked if the Defiant is that bad. Well, it's bad enough for us to be switched to night flying..." He seemed to notice the expression on Gus's face. "Oh, didn't they tell you? The squadron was beaten up so badly in daylight, we've been redesignated a night fighter unit. You'd better get used to the bugger in daylight before the squadron starts night training in earnest. Climb in, Bouncer."

The turret, which housed four .303 Browning machine guns, was mounted immediately behind the pilot's cockpit. It was transverse, across the aeroplane's fuselage, with the guns on the starboard side. This exposed, on the port side, two sliding panels — the entrance to the turret. Gus climbed up and wriggled into the turret.

"When I start the engine, you use that lever —" Marten pointed it out — "to move the turret to face forwards; that's the take-off, cruising and landing position. The guns shouldn't be armed, but don't bloody well touch them just in case, will you?"

Marten climbed into the cockpit and strapped himself in. Once at the controls and with the checks done, he gave a sign to a mechanic and the engine started second pull. He jazzed it for half a minute to make sure it was warmed up.

"Sound good?" he asked, over the intercom.

"Sounds wonderful."

"So it bloody well ought. It's the same Rolls-Royce Merlin as the Spits and Hurricanes have. Only, it's got so much more work to do with all this extra baggage. Right, move the turret round with that lever I showed you."

"Roger," said Gus. The hydraulics whirred as the four-gun turret moved around.

"Now lower the guns."

"Roger that."

Marten raised the movable fairings, which were mounted between cockpit and turret and behind the turret, to give the Daffy a more aerodynamic shape in flight. He opened the throttle and the Defiant picked up speed along the grassy runway. Marten pulled back on the joystick, raising the nose of the aircraft into the sky. Gus noted its modest rate of climb. It was not an aircraft to be caught in by 109s at take-off, he thought.

"What do I need to know?" he asked.

"First, the Daffy isn't a dogfighter, so don't tangle with any 109s or 110s."

"What if I get bounced by enemy fighters?"

"A few months ago, 264 Squadron's CO flew a trial in a Daffy against Bob Stanford Tuck as an experiment," said Marten.

"Stanford Tuck, the Ace?"

"One and the same. He was flying a Spitfire."

"How did it go?"

"Well, it was far from a complete disaster. Hunter, that's 264's CO, proved the Daffy could defend itself against fighters. The trick is to lose height, circle and keep the speed up. Yes, we sacrifice the advantage of height, but we eliminate the possibility of attack from below, and we give the turret gunner a full 360 degree field of fire. That way, your gunner can hold off any forward-firing fighter. Pity our own lads didn't use the same tactic when we were bounced by those 109s. Poor old Jimmy hated the idea. Look what happened to him. We lost seven out of nine aircraft."

Marten banked to starboard.

"So, you may be unlucky enough to be attacked by a German fighter at night," he said. "But it's very unlikely, I'd say. If you are, descend as low as possible and fly round and round the smallest circular course you can manage. Do that until you run out of either ammo or petrol."

"Or until Jerry gets fed up! Fantastic!" said Gus.

"Second," Marten went on, in full flow now, "the Daffy is suited, I'd say, to bomber-destroyer duties. After all, that's what the bloody thing was designed for. To be fair on them, the Daffies may be a bloody nightmare in daylight, but I think they might just turn out to be much better suited to the night-fighter role. You need to remember it's slow, got that?"

"Roger that."

"You need to approach the bomber from behind — always from behind. Then stay underneath the bloody thing if you can — get a good long shot at his belly."

"Roger," said Gus.

"Third, your gunner will do all the work. What he needs is a steady platform to shoot from. That's down to you. Got it?"

"Got it. Thanks, Pine."

As they flew back to West Malling, Gus had just one thing on his mind. How the bloody hell was he going to fly a Defiant to France and back without alerting the rear gunner to what was going on?

Though the atmosphere on the base was generally relaxed and friendly, training was intensive. The next day Gus took a Defiant up alone and put himself through the paces: take-off, landing, level flying, evasive action.

A few days later he began gunnery training and met Mike Murphy, an Irish airman in his mid-twenties who was new to the squadron. Nicknamed 'Spud', he had been posted as Gus's gunner.

Gus found Murphy easy to work with. He was a serious man who seemed not to take fools lightly. He was also diligent and a stickler for getting things right.

"Just one thing, Spud," Gus said before their first flight together.

"Yes, Skip?"

"Each and every time we are about to land, I want you to ask me if I have put the landing gear down. Understood?"

"Understood," said a very worried-looking Murphy. "Please may I ask why, Skipper?"

"Yes, you may. I've only been flying aircraft with retractable undercarriages for a couple of weeks, and I'm bloody terrified that one day I might forget to put the wheels down! That's between you and me, right?"

"Right."

"And it doesn't make me a bad pilot — I just want to be sure!"

They repeatedly practised attacking Bristol Blenheim and Handley Page Hampden medium bombers. The pair followed the general instruction and attacked the target bombers from below, concentrating on communications between themselves on the intercom.

"Here we go again," said Gus as he approached a Hampden half a mile in front of them. "Ready?"

"I'm ready."

Gus concentrated on keeping the Daffy steady and level as he approached the Hampden. In the turret, Murphy awaited his opportunity, then...

"Bang! Got him, Skipper. Shot his sodding tailplane off," said Murphy.

Gus turned for home.

"But it won't work on operations, Skip," said Murphy, once they were back on the ground and debriefing over a cup of tea.

"Why not?"

"Can I speak my mind, sir?"

"Of course. Go ahead."

"Well, those Hampden pilots have been told to keep a steady course and speed as we're attacking them. The Luftwaffe will take evasive action as soon as they sense we're onto them. We need to shoot earlier. As it is, I can't shoot until the Daffy has caught the bugger up — or overtaken it for a really good shot. Even then I'm shooting his tail, whereas it would be better shooting at his engines or up into his belly."

He's right, thought Gus. "Well, what do you suggest?" he asked, and Murphy explained his ideas.

The following day the pair were in the skies again, going through much the same gunnery training. As they closed in on a Hampden, Gus was on the intercom. "I'm going to try getting in close on his port side. You ready? Swing the turret to your left."

"Roger." Murphy operated the hydraulic mechanism that moved the turret, bringing it around ninety degrees to his left so that the guns faced the side of the Hampden.

"Ready, Skipper," he said.

"Here we go! Tally-ho!"

Gus concentrated on keeping the Defiant steady. Murphy waited for the Hampden to appear in his sights.

"Bang, bang, bang! Got him, Skip!" he announced triumphantly.

"Bloody marvellous," said Gus. "Even an experienced pilot in a fast and nimble Dornier wouldn't get away from us!"

"Hope not, Skip."

Within a week, this method was adopted by the whole squadron.

Training at night began towards the end of June, and at the same time the squadron's Defiants were painted black.

Gus found the basics a little different from day flying. He'd take off, give Murphy a level platform from which to shoot, then land — remembering to lower the undercarriage first.

Finding his way around was the hardest aspect of night fighter flying.

An operational sortie would go something like this: when ground-based radar picked up an attacking force in their sector, a squadron, or part of it, would be scrambled and given a course to fly. This course would take them to a point where ground-based searchlights would illuminate the attackers. That was the theory. Finding the attackers was far from straightforward. The tactic was for both pilot and air-gunner to keep a lookout for a bomber illuminated by these ground-based searchlights, and it helped that one of them was facing backwards. Of course, Luftwaffe pilots would do all they could to escape the searchlight.

The pilots' manual said a Daffy could carry enough fuel to spend one hour forty-five minutes in the air. Gus, like all the other pilots in the squadron, knew this was an absolute maximum in ideal cruising conditions. In practice, in took about ten minutes to take off and gain altitude, and perhaps another fifteen to reach the interception zone. They also needed to allow twenty minutes, or thirty to be safe, to get back and land. Gus needed to time how long they were in the zone looking for and shooting at the Luftwaffe whilst keeping a close eye on the fuel gauge. After around forty minutes of searching and possibly fighting, he would break off the sortie and turn for home.

Then he would try to find West Malling airfield on instruments and in total darkness. First, using the gyro compass, Gus would fly on a course to take him to the vicinity of Malling. Once in the general area of the base, Gus then had to find the runway. It went without saying that during a blackout the runway lights would not be on. The instrument landing system that used the Defiant's wireless was a big help. It would get them within half a mile of the runway at two hundred feet if used correctly. Then it was down to Gus to spot the sparsely distributed, gloomy landing lights that were lit only when a Daffy pilot broke radio silence to indicate he was ready to make an approach.

The first time Gus made a night landing was under a full moon in early July. It went almost perfectly, though it was a little lively upon contact with the ground.

The squadron quickly progressed to night-time gunnery training, which all the crews found gruelling. One dark, murky night following a solid hour of looking for a Blenheim that had kept dodging the searchlight, Gus brought the Daffy in, the altitude dial showing height above ground level: five hundred feet, four-fifty feet, four hundred feet. Flaps down.

"Base, base, base! This is Red Gee, Red Gee, over," Gus said into the RT.

"Receiving you loud and clear, over," came the distorted reply into his earphones.

"Approaching at three-fifty feet, permission to land, over."

"Lights on now — down you come, Bouncer. Over."

He saw dimmed lights indicating the runway, but they were two hundred yards away to his left. Bugger! He opened the throttle, fully regained height, circled and approached the base again.

He watched the instruments, one eye constantly on the altitude dial: five hundred feet, four-fifty feet, four hundred feet. Flaps down.

"Red Gee to base, Red Gee to base, over," said Gus.

"Come on, Bouncer, get her on the right bloody course. Lights on now. Over."

Two-fifty feet, two hundred feet.

"Landing gear! Landing gear, Skipper!" yelled Murphy.

Gus opened the throttle fully yet again, regained height and went through the whole procedure for a third time. He watched the altitude dial: two hundred feet, landing gear down; one-fifty feet, one hundred feet, fifty feet… *Thump*! Up the Daffy went, the wings severely tilting. Then down again, with a thud.

CHAPTER 13

Gus felt he owed Murphy a thank you, so he decided to treat the young Irishman to a drink or two in their local, The Bull, in West Malling.

"What will you have, Spud?" he asked.

Murphy looked around the bar and spotted some white wine. "Glass of that, please."

Gus ordered and the landlord pulled a foaming pint of Kentish beer and a glass of white wine.

"Here's to you, to us and to shooting down as many Luftwaffe kites as we can," said Gus, holding up his glass of beer.

"I'll drink to that," said Murphy, a smile on his usually serious face.

"Thanks for that warning last night. I hadn't put the bloody wheels down. We'd have crashed for sure."

"I know. I can always hear the undercarriage going down and feel the extra drag. Don't worry about it, Skipper. We'd had a difficult night."

Gus thought he'd try to find out a little more about his faithful gunner. "Which part of Ireland are you from?"

"Offaly. Used to be called the King's County, before independence, that is."

"That's an odd choice of drink for an Irishman, if you don't mind me saying so."

"Oh, this?" Murphy glanced at his wine. "I suppose. I developed a taste for it during the Spanish Civil War."

"You fought there?"

"I did, so."

"Tell me about it, then."

Over a second, then a third glass of wine, Murphy related the tale of his time in Spain.

"The Connolly Column marched — some might say we marched badly — but we marched towards the Jarama valley. Irish volunteers were in the thick of it. Boy, were we hot! My throat was parched from the dusty Spanish roads. I grasped for my water bottle, but it was empty. A volunteer called O'Leary called over to me and handed me a skin of liquid. I put to my lips. It was wine. Cool, refreshing, white wine. Better than this plonk," he said, taking a sip of his wine with a smile.

"Most of us Irish who fought in Spain alongside the government forces served in one company: La Quince Brigada — the Fifteenth International Brigade. Connolly Column was the name we gave ourselves — after James Connolly, the leader of the Irish Citizen Army in the Easter Rising. You've heard of him, I expect?"

"Hardly," replied Gus. "I wasn't born in 1916, and the Irish rebellion hasn't made the history books. Yet."

"Rebellion? Rebellion, you call it? It was the beginning of a revolution. Connolly was executed by the British for his part in it. He was worshipped by the Irish volunteers of La Quince Brigada. Respected as an Irishman, and as a socialist."

"You're a socialist, then?"

"Aye, I am so and proud of it. But let me carry on with the story, will you?"

"Sorry, go on."

"Well, us volunteers of the Connolly Column and Fifteenth International Brigade marched to the Jarama, a river a few miles east of Madrid. We were to attack the Fascists. We knew they were strong. They had the Army of Africa spearheaded by Spanish Legionnaires and Moroccan regulars. But we had time before any fighting started. I got to know O'Leary. I asked him how he got involved. He said his story was like most of ours. He was angry. He hated the thought of a military takeover of an elected socialist Republic, especially a takeover backed by Italy and Germany. So, he took a boat to Spain with some other lads and joined in. O'Leary had been told we'd got about fifty Soviet T-26 tanks with us, and artillery support, decent air cover. Sure, we were ready to beat the hell out of the Fascist bastards, so we were.

"What O'Leary had been told about our weaponry was true enough, but it didn't match that of the Fascists. We took a severe battering at Jamara, suffering horrendously. You see, Skipper, we were keen enough, but we were inexperienced, and there was little training. So we advanced without adequate artillery or air support. We were gunned down. Butchered.

"Same thing happened again during the following summer, when the Brigade attempted to relieve the siege of Madrid by attacking at Brunete. We lost twenty-five thousand men and a hundred aircraft. Altogether, I spent two years in Spain. It was hopeless! I went back to Ireland in March thirty-nine."

"Crikey. You've really been through it!" exclaimed Gus. "That's real devotion. I applaud you." He paused, thinking. He contemplated his drink and fidgeted with his glass before blurting out, "You said you're a socialist, Spud. Are you a communist?"

The Irishman thought as he took a large sip of white wine. "Why do you ask?" he asked.

"Well — this is just between you and me, right?"

"Sure, Skipper. You can trust me."

"The thing is, I want to know more because … because I think my mother might be a Red."

"Your mother? Well, as I see it there's nothing wrong with being a communist. I met many of them in Spain. Some Spanish, some volunteers. And the Russians, of course. No. I'm not a communist. I'm a socialist. Communism has a bad name because of Stalin. No, I'm certainly not one of them. What about you? What are your politics?"

"Bit of a liberal, I suppose."

Murphy shrugged. "Sorry, I find it difficult to understand non-commitment."

Gus flushed a little. "Why do you think the Republicans failed in Spain?"

"The Fascists were too bloody strong, that's the main thing. They were well supported by Germany and Italy, and they were much better supplied. The only government to support the Republicans were the Soviets. It really is a disgrace, you know, that Ireland, Britain and France didn't lend a hand. Once the Fascists controlled the main ports and France wouldn't allow aid across the border, it became much more difficult to supply the Republican armies. So that's one reason." Murphy drank more wine. "For me, the main problem was that the left just wasn't united."

After another swig, Murphy's glass was empty. Gus re-charged both their drinks.

"The Marxist Workers Party was denounced by other communists as an instrument of fascism. Outrageous! Eventually thousands of anarchists and communists were fighting each other for control of strategic points in Barcelona."

"Sounds like a bloody mess to me," said Gus.

"It was a bloody mess!"

"Is that why you came to fight alongside us?" asked Gus.

"It's not so much fighting with you, it's more fighting against fascism. I fought them in Spain, and I'll fight them again. I came to England to have another pop at the Germans."

"Why did you choose the air force over the army?"

"I saw what damage those Fascist bomber planes did. Their tactic was aerial bombing of cities in Republican-held territory. Madrid, Barcelona, Valencia, they were all bombed. The bastards deliberately targeted residential areas, shopping areas. It was mainly done by Luftwaffe volunteers in the Condor Legion and the Italians. Guernica was the most controversial."

"Yes, it was all over the papers," said Gus.

"Where were you liberals then? Sorry."

"No. Go on."

"They killed more than seventeen hundred people. The town was ruined. When this war broke out, I decided the best contribution I could make was to help shoot the Nazi bastards out of the sky!"

"I have to say, Spud, I do admire your passion."

"What about you, Skipper? Why did you join up?"

"I always wanted to fly. While you were fighting in Spain, I was studying History at Oxford. I was two years into a three-year degree when the war broke out. I began flying in October 1937 at a club, so I was already a qualified pilot. The RAF was obvious. I did think about the Navy — always fancied taking off and landing on carriers."

Murphy nearly choked on his wine. "My God, no! The way you go about landings, you'd end up in the drink!"

Gus smiled and downed more beer.

"Do you know what I worry about most when I'm flying along in a Daffy?" Murphy asked in a more serious tone.

"I can guess. You worry that if we're hit, you won't get out of that blasted turret. You worry that I'll be able to bail out, but you won't. You worry you're going to burn to death."

"Exactly. There wouldn't be a chance of survival, would there?"

"There's always a chance," said Gus.

A month later, all crews had negotiated the night-flying classes and were informed that they were to be deployed on active night fighter operations. Murphy and the other gunners in the squadron received the additional good news that they were all being promoted to Sergeant Aircrew, in recognition of the dangerous duties they were undertaking.

Acting Squadron Leader Holbrook gathered the officers for a celebratory drink in the mess. "Many, many congratulations to all of you," he said. "Without a doubt, every one of you, and your crews, have worked hard and deserve this success. But make no mistake: from now on, things are going to get much more serious. The Luftwaffe is stepping up its night-time raids, and it's our job to stop them. Remember, get up there fast, give your gunners a steady platform and let them have it! Oh, and a special mention goes to one of you. So special, in fact, that I am moved to verse."

Holbrook took a small piece of paper and a pencil from his pocket. When the room fell silent, he read:

"A budding night flyer called Bouncer,
Had a troubling off-course encounter.
Back on track with good luck
But undercarriage up.
'Wheels down!' cried his back-seat announcer."

PART THREE: THE BATTLE OF BRITAIN

CHAPTER 14

Gus had a hand in his cousin's re-posting. He took advantage of a meeting with Peacock at the RAF Club to raise the subject. Squadron Leader Taylor was, as Gus predicted, also present.

"Look," he said, "Pilot Officer Rosen is an experienced fighter pilot. He fought in Poland and downed a number of superior German aircraft. He also downed a Dornier in France."

Peacock looked unconvinced. "Stuffy doesn't rate the Poles," he said.

Taylor looked confused.

"Stuffy Dowding, the boss," Peacock clarified. "At a top-level meeting a few weeks ago, he stated that regardless of their previous experience, all Polish pilots would be most useful if transferred to Bomber Command."

"Does the Air Marshal need to know?" asked Taylor.

Peacock frowned at the Polish officer. "Stuffy isn't stupid. Far from it. He is well aware that British factories are now in full swing turning out more and more Hurries and Spits by the week. Our young pilots are being pushed rapidly through the training regime. Soon the Luftwaffe will be in the skies over southern England, and the RAF will be in action fighting them. Fighter Command will inevitably begin to suffer aircraft losses and pilot casualties. So, how to utilise the Polish and Czech pilots recently arrived from France? He considers all this. Only the other day the Air Marshal travelled to Eastchurch, where a group of Polish pilots were billeted. He told me he wasn't looking forward to it because the Poles had a poor reputation.

Their air force was destroyed by the Luftwaffe in a matter of days last September."

"That's totally unfair, Sir Alex," said Taylor. "Our planes were caught on the ground, just as the French were in May."

"Besides Pilot Officer Rosen being a top fighter pilot," said Gus, bringing the conversation back to the matter at hand, "his English is excellent. He'll fit in well with a British squadron, sir."

It was probably Staś Rosen's near perfect English which clinched his posting to a Spitfire squadron based at RAF Biggin Hill in Kent, British command being wary of pilots who didn't speak English.

Staś saw action in the early days of the great air battle which was beginning to unfold. In July, he and Gus had a bit of leave and had arranged to meet in London. Staś sat before his cousin, looking smart in an RAF uniform with the Polish Air Force eagle as his cap badge and a 'Poland' flash on his shoulder.

"How is it going?" asked Gus.

"It's frantic. Bloody frantic."

"Start at the beginning, hey?"

"Following some pretty basic training in ground control and navigational equipment, we started combat training. It's so bloody frustrating," said Staś. "I sat in a classroom and was indoctrinated into RAF practices by a training officer called Nielsen, a thirty-something-year-old who I suspect had never seen action. The RAF is bound by its own regulations and fly-by-the-book procedures. When we took off, it was in a very tight V formation. When we fought it was the same, close Vs with leader and wingman. I told them, in Poland we were trained to fly in loose, fluid patterns. 'Really?' said Nielsen. 'And you lasted, what? Three days, was it?' Bastard!"

"You just have to ignore that sort of talk."

"Seriously, how do they expect us to look out for Messerschmitts when we've got our hands full just trying to avoid each other's wingtips?"

"It's the RAF way of doing things," said Gus.

"That's what Nielsen said. It's bloody nonsense. How can we possibly react lightning-quick when we are virtually wing tip to bloody wing tip with each other? Neilsen didn't want to know. 'Let's move on,' he said, and explained that our first operational role would be as a wingman to a more experienced pilot. He explained the wingman's role: our responsibility is to remain close to the leader, stick to him like glue and warn him of any immediate threats, especially above and below him. I had my hand raised, and he let me ask my question."

"And what did you ask him?"

"I said, 'Have I got this correct? I have to stick to him like glue, which means looking forwards at him whilst also keeping a lookout for the enemy above and behind him?'"

"What did Nielsen say to that?"

"He said that was correct. 'At three hundred knots?' I asked. Do you know what the bastard said?"

"Go on."

"He said, in that condescending voice of his, 'Oh, a little faster, but you've never flown at that sort of speed, have you?' Pompous bastard. *I'll bloody show you*, I thought.

"At last I took a Spitfire up for the first time. That once was good enough for the instructors to sign me off. On my second flight in a Spit, I buzzed the airfield at treetop level and followed it up with a downwind victory roll. Nielsen was livid!"

"You mustn't cause them too much grief, Staś."

"On my first sortie with the new squadron at Biggin Hill, I was assigned as tail-end Charlie. I didn't like it. It was like being the wingman for a whole flight of Spitfires. I knew that I was the easiest target for any roaming Messerschmitt, without anyone looking out for me.

"We took off in that tight V formation — oh, I'm sure it looked magnificent from the ground. Once we'd climbed up to eighteen thousand feet, I began squinting and scanning the skies and was the first to spot some Bf-109s approaching from the direction of France. They were buzzing around a group of Heinkel bombers. *This is it*, I thought. *At last.* 'Bandits three o'clock, Angels fifteen thousand,' I radioed to the others. The squadron leader's a chap called Tiny Wilson. Know of him?"

"No."

"Well, he came back quickly over the RT. 'Follow me, go after the fighters,' he ordered. 'Tally-ho!' *That's good*, I thought. At least the British were ready to be aggressive, not like the bloody French.

"As I dived towards the group of German planes, I spotted four other aircraft coming from the opposite direction — more 109s. So I quickly changed direction and headed straight into the oncoming flight of four Germans. I sent a barrage of .303 bullets forwards, immediately breaking up the small group. Three of them disappeared, but one wanted to fight. *Come on then, you Nazi bastard*, I thought. Got any more Scotch, Gus?"

Gus went to fetch more drink, briefly leaving Staś with his memories. Once his drink had been poured, Staś continued his tale.

"Then we were caught in our own micro war, diving, banking and rolling through the blue skies. It felt like an eternity. That 109 dived towards the sea, but I was after him. Then he pulled up at the last minute and headed towards the white cliffs, almost touching the waves as he tried to evade me. But I could feel the Spitfire was gaining on him. As the 109 climbed to clear the cliffs, I closed range and opened fire with those eight Browning machine guns. He flipped to port and exploded, splattering my windscreen with oil. I flew back to Biggin Hill exhausted, and reported the kill to the CO later that day. He congratulated me and told me that getting my first kill on my first sortie was quite a thing."

Staś starred at Gus. "You know it wasn't my first sortie, Gus. You know I flew two sorties every day in the first four days of the German invasion of Poland. Sometimes more. And even more in France, but that was boring. As for kills, I downed two German bombers over Poland, both of them Heinkel 111s, and a Dornier in France. Tiny Wilson didn't know. He ought to have, so I told him that it was actually my fourth kill. But it was my first Messerschmitt 109, so it was to be celebrated. That took the wind out of his sails.

"I soon discovered that I was one of the most experienced combat pilots in the squadron. Soon I was leading a section of three Spitfires. Our biggest problem is the very few hours of flying experience in Spits that the incoming young pilots have. As section leader, I'm often having to do the job of a flying instructor. Not that the Spit is a particularly difficult aeroplane to fly. It's easy, actually, though not as forgiving as the P-11, perhaps. But it has some issues."

"I hope to fly one, one of these days. Give me the detail, as much as you can. I'll decide what to commit to memory."

"You want detail? Then here we go: the Spit's air-intake is set behind the undercarriage, so they're prone to overheating prior to take-off. Especially if the pilot waits around too long. On the runway and into take-off there's a lot of work to be done. There's a massive prop torque created by that powerful Merlin engine, so you need to be ready to push your right foot forward for full right rudder in order to counteract the swing effect from it. Once in the air, the ailerons can be sticky. The Spit's bubble canopy and large mirrors give the pilot excellent views, great for situational awareness, so long as you make full use of it. But these young kids, oh. Many of them have never been in combat before. They either learn quick or die quick.

"They tend to open up five hundred metres away from the target. Useless. I had two rookie pilots in my section — Pilot Officer Jake Wendover and Flight Sergeant George Avery. Good pilots, but raw. After one sortie, I sat them down for a debriefing. 'Tell me,' I said, 'in training, what did they say about firing distances? When should you open fire?' Wendover answered first. 'Five hundred yards,' he said. 'Well,' I told him, 'that's all right for a slow-moving bomber giving you a big target to shoot at. But you can forget it for a 109 or 110.' I told them they must get in much closer before opening up. 'It's got to be under three hundred yards to down a German fighter,' I said. They looked incredulous. I said that we'd see how it went the next day.

"Then I went to see the armourer, a chief technician, Sergeant Davies. I asked him how the guns were harmonised. He said that regulations call for six hundred yards and pattern harmonisation. It's a bit like a shotgun; it disperses the fire of the eight guns to gain a greater chance of a hit.

"I told him to alter the harmonisation of the three Spits in Red section to two hundred yards. He complained that it was most irregular, but he followed my order. We were scrambled the following day. We were on the runway within minutes. Racing across the ground, I eased the throttle forward to the gate to engage full power. Now I was at seventy-four knots, or what I thought to be about one hundred and forty kilometres per hour. I still think in kilometres, you know. Funny, that, isn't it?"

"Hilarious," said Gus. "Get on with the bloody story before I fall asleep."

"Once up to speed, I looked in the mirror to see Avery and Wendover behind me, then climbed to four thousand metres. 'Red one to Red section, follow me to rendezvous,' I ordered. 'I'll show you how we get close enough for a one-burst kill.'

"Our job was basically to engage the German escort fighter aeroplanes that accompanied Nazi bombers, allowing those RAF squadrons equipped with slower Hurricanes to attack the bombers. Of course, it didn't always work out according to plan. Today I was determined it wouldn't. I needed my rookies to learn on the slower bombers of the Luftwaffe. Circling at six thousand metres, I soon picked out a group of eight Heinkel He-111s below us without any obvious fighter escort. 'Red section, keep your height and circle me,' I said, 'and keep a lookout for any fighters.'

"I brought my Spitfire out of the sun and in a steep dive aimed at the flank of the attacking bombers. I got within three hundred yards and opened fire, raking the flank of the bomber stream with .303 ammo. As I half rolled on the break, I saw one of the Heinkels slide out of line, enter a steep dive and disappear into the cloud. Turning rapidly to starboard, I came around again and attacked the leading He-111, watching the tracer stream into its side. I broke away through a layer of cloud and picked out a single bomber heading south below. I went into a stern chase and caught up with the enemy Heinkel. My opening burst, again at very close range, caused the bomber to dive away, smoke pluming from its port engine. The small formation was broken up and I left it, re-joining the rest of Red section at a higher altitude. Wendover and Avery congratulated me and asked if it was their turn next. I checked my fuel levels and the time. *Yes,* I thought, *let's find another target.*"

"Sounds like a successful sortie."

"I was lambasted for it," said Staś. "Wendover reported a Ju-88 down and Avery claimed he winged another. But Wilson didn't approve. He asked if we'd really shot down three Heinkels and a Ju-88. I confirmed that we had. Then he queried why there were no fighters around. I told him I hadn't encountered any. He said Yellow section had been punched by two 110s, but they didn't see much of us. I replied that I hadn't seen much of Yellow section. Then Tiny got on his high horse and asked what I was up to. Sergeant Davies had told him I'd had the harmonisation changed on Red section's planes, and he asked me if that was true."

"You do get yourself into trouble, Staś," offered Gus. "What did you say?"

"I said I had, to set the harmonisation at a closer range. He told me it wasn't in the regulations, but I argued that it seemed to work." Staś laughed. "Tiny Wilson was livid with me. 'Dismissed!' he shouted. I went to the mess for some food, then up to my room. What is it about these fuddy-duddies? Why can't they see sense? I just want to forget about it all."

CHAPTER 15

The Defiant was on the runway, engine roaring and ready to go. Gus felt for the weighted package he had secreted away from Spud Murphy's sight, stuffed under his life vest. It was there, safe. With the cockpit canopy still open, Gus could feel the cold of the night air. He had spoken to Osborn, the NCO at West Malling airfield in charge of the small team of mechanics who serviced her.

"Did you find the problem affecting the compass?" he asked.

"Couldn't find nothing wrong, sir," the airman had told him.

"It must be some electrical fault."

"Sorry, sir, we can't find anything wrong. See how she goes this time."

In the rear turret, Murphy had personally overseen the loading of belts of .303 ammo into the four Browning machine guns. Now he manually loaded the first round of each belt into each gun's chamber.

"Ready for take-off?" asked Gus through the intercom.

"Ready!"

"Chocks away!"

Gus opened the throttle and the Merlin boomed. The Daffy bumped its way along the grassy strip, slowly at first but gathering speed then rising into the air. Their instructions were to take off into the moderate easterly wind and turn south, flying at five thousand feet over Ashford to intercept a formation of German aircraft picked up on radar. Hopefully, they would meet the enemy over Romney Marsh. The crews didn't know what aircraft they were flying off to intercept, as the ground-based observers couldn't operate effectively at night. Gus reasoned they were most likely to be Dornier Do-17s, as these had been encountered recently. Not that it mattered.

It didn't matter for two reasons. First, because the squadron's tactics were pretty much the same whatever type of bomber they encountered — Dorniers, Heinkels or Junkers Ju-88s. Gus would select a target, approach from behind and get to one side of the bomber or the other and slightly underneath. Then he would focus on giving Murphy a steady firing platform. If they encountered Bf-110s, on the other hand, they would turn away and hurry home.

The second reason it really didn't matter what type of Luftwaffe aeroplane they encountered was simple: Gus had no intention of intercepting them. Instead, he was resolved to carry out Peacock's orders to see whether it was possible to fly from southern England into occupied France at night. He decided that doing so during an ordinary night fighter operation was probably the best way to avoid attracting attention.

Gus kept the throttle open, lifted the undercarriage and banked to starboard to pick up his southerly course. He levelled off at five thousand feet and looked below. It was too murky to see anything. Good. Murphy would have no way of knowing that they weren't heading south. They were on a course of 140 degrees, a south-easterly course that would take them over Cap Gris Nez and on into French airspace.

Peacock wanted him to review the possibility of night landings and take-offs from small fields in Nazi-occupied France. That meant flying very low. When he thought they were halfway across the Channel, Gus reduced the engine revs and started to lose height.

"Problem, Skipper?"

"Compass has packed up. It's the electrics again. Osborn assured me he'd got it sorted. He knows the bloody gyro compass is liable to trip out if there's a power failure."

"That bloody ground crew," said Murphy. "What a shambles!"

"I'm not sure where we are. I'm going to fly lower to try to find a landmark. Keep your eyes peeled, too."

He lost height and approached the French coast at a ridiculously low five hundred feet, but at least this meant he could clearly make out the distinctive shape of the cape.

The sky behind them exploded in light and the Daffy shuddered as shells exploded close by.

"What in God's name is that?" shouted Murphy.

"British flak," replied Gus, not wanting Spud to realise they were over the French coast. "Good job they're poor shots.

More flak exploded in the air, but far behind them. Clearly they had taken the German gunners on the coast by surprise.

Gus made a series of zigzags over the low-lying landscape, surveying the fields, hedges and the general lie of the land. To the left was a farmhouse with a number of outbuildings. He pointed the Daffy at them. Still flying very low in the night sky, Gus opened up the cockpit and flung out the weighted package.

Then, gaining height rapidly, he glanced at the compass on the cockpit floor. He picked up the reciprocal bearing — 280 degrees, a heading that would take them close enough to base to enable him to use the instrument landing system and the Defiant's wireless.

When Gus made it back to base, he was immediately summoned by Squadron Leader Holbrook. "This report is absolute nonsense, Bouncer," said the CO, once Gus had given his fabricated account of what had happened. "What do you mean, you had no idea where you were?"

"Compass malfunction. I had reported it."

"Osborn tells me there isn't a problem with the aircraft or its electrics."

"It's my job to fly the plane, sir, not to maintain it. I can only report what I find."

"Now, now. No need for that, Bouncer."

"Sorry, no need for what?"

"The 'sir'!"

"Sorry, no offence. Look, Keats, all I know is the compass packed up. Why they can't fit a bloody magnetic compass into the Daffy I really don't know."

"Sergeant Murphy thinks you were flying over France."

"Really?"

"Yes, he does. Were you?"

"No idea, Keats. Bloody compass packed up!"

"So you say. Look, Bouncer, I don't like doing this…"

"But?"

"But you're off flying ops until we sort this out. Sorry, old fellow."

A few days after the mission Peacock summoned Gus to the RAF Club. This time, however, they had a private room. "I followed the whole operation on radar," said Peacock.

"You did?"

"Yes. A young flight lieutenant called Warner had the bad luck of being the duty controller at the Intruder Operations room that night. It's at Bentley Priory — nice place. Anyway, Warner talked me through it. He looked like he hated the job. Bad enough being up all bloody night, but briefing a bloody wing commander from the PM's office! Why, oh why did these things have to happen to him? That's what he was thinking, I'm sure. At least he had the company of two WAAFs who plotted the positions of German bomber formations onto a gigantic map. Warner introduced them as Dotty and Joyce, but I digress. It was Warner's job to phone up the squadrons so they could scramble RAF fighters to intercept them."

"Mind me asking your cover story?"

"Oh, you are learning fast, aren't you, Gustaw? I just told him we needed to see how the system worked. Warner couldn't seem to tear his eyes away from those busy WAAFs. Then there was the wireless 'noise' man who seemed to have trouble staying awake. Anyway, Warner was talking me through it all. Their job, he told me, is to find the bases the Luftwaffe are operating from and order off our long-range night fighters to attack them at the time they are due to land. I watched as the WAAFs monitored and plotted the flight paths of numerous aeroplanes on the map. It was bloody fascinating. I saw a flight take off from Malling and move towards Faversham. Was that you?"

"What sort of time are we talking about?"

"0400, I think."

"Yes, then. Probably us."

"The WAAFs busied themselves and the Malling flight turned south, heading to intercept a Luftwaffe formation that was still crossing the Channel. All was carefully mapped before my very eyes.

"As they neared the Germans, one aircraft from the Malling flight peeled away and headed over the Channel. It was you, my good man. Nobody else seemed to notice. Why should they? Once it was isolated, over the English coast and heading in the general direction of Calais, I pointed and drew attention to it. 'What's that?' I asked Warner. He told me it was likely that one of the enemy had picked up an engine issue and was returning to base. Too sure of himself, that one. Anyway, he promptly lost interest in the lone aircraft in favour of Dotty. Or was it Joyce? Fifteen or twenty minutes later, the various combatants from the melee over Romney Marsh began to disengage and return to their respective bases. I noticed a lone aircraft crossing the Channel in the opposite direction. I pointed to it. 'What's that one?' I asked. Warner said it must be one of ours. He thought the pilot must have pursued Jerry to get a definite kill to paint on his kite, and now he was coming home.

"Warner turned once again to the WAAF, and she smiled at him. Oh, to be young and think you're going to die before the end of the month."

There was a knock at the door.

"Ah, that'll be our guest," said Peacock. He stood up and opened the door. "Larry, so good of you to come," he said, then turned to Gus. "Allow me to introduce Pilot Officer Hislop, though I believe you may have met before?"

As usual, Peacock knew everything. Gus stood up and shook hands with his former flying instructor.

"So, you're back in uniform, Larry," he said.

"Let's have a sit down, and you two can catch up," suggested Peacock. "I'll get us some drinks." He left the room.

"I'm back in uniform, yes," said Hislop. "With the war and everything, I enlisted with the Royal Air Force Volunteer Reserve in 1939. I went in as a sergeant pilot and I've been flying Spits. Beautiful kites. I was shot down in one over France, as a matter of fact. I just got back, actually."

"Bloody hell, how?"

"I manged to keep my head down where Jerry was concerned and eventually hooked up with the Resistance. They got me out by boat. Would have been a lot better to have flown out. That's where you come in, actually, old boy."

Peacock came back with drinks. "You two have updated yourselves, then?" He looked at Gus. "There's no point in beating about the bush. The PM is in favour of helping and developing resistance movements in Europe — France, the Low Countries, Greece. Winnie's aim is two-fold. In his words, we need to develop a spirit of resistance in the Nazi-occupied countries, and to develop a fifth column of resistance fighters to assist in the liberation of their countries at some future point, when we British will return. Now, to support these aims, we need a system of communication and supply to the Resistance. Larry, as I'm sure he's told you, has been over there. He thinks the RAF should be involved. Larry?"

"We need to be able to fly over there. We need to land messages, messengers, supplies and agents. And we need to pick up agents, pilots, the odd bottle of plonk, if we're lucky, and get them back to Blighty."

"That's why I asked you to do the job for us, Gustaw."

"Asked me? I thought it was an order."

"Yes, asked. This is all unofficial. I can't order you; you know that by now. So what did you find?"

"It's easy enough to get over there," said Gus. "There are two ways. You can either get mixed up with a formation of returning Jerries, or go in alone. If the latter, you go in very low."

"That's the way," said Hislop. "What about landing? And take-off?"

"Pick your aircraft and it's possible."

"Any suggestions?"

"A Lysander would do it. Given reasonably level, firm ground, a Lysander can land and take off on a one-hundred-yard strip. A bit less, I suppose."

"And the navigation?"

"I didn't have far to go," said Gus. "I worked out a plan using compass bearings with a good landmark, Cap Gris Nez. Some moonlight helps, that's for sure. I'd say you need good pilots and very good navigators."

"But there's no room in a Lizzie for a navigator, not if you are dropping off or picking people up," said Hislop.

"Then we'll need to find good pilots who are very good navigators," said Peacock. "Or train them! By the way, Gustaw, I hear you hit a spot of bother with Keats over at Malling?"

"More than a bloody spot of bother, I'd say. I'm grounded."

"Don't worry about that. I've got another posting for you. Much more exciting. How do you fancy a secondment as a translator with an all-Polish fighter squadron?"

"Night fighters?"

"No, Hurricanes. You'd be based on the edge of London, in the thick of it."

"Why me?"

"Why not you? I think Stuffy Dowding's having a change of heart regarding the Polish pilots. About bloody time, in my opinion. He lost three hundred fighter pilots in France and he's losing more day on day as this battle progresses. He's decided to hurry things up. We're close to mobilising all Polish fighter pilots. Those previously on bomber duty will be re-assigned; we should have done it months ago. Still, better late than never. He's even up for forming some all-Polish units — well, with a Czech or two, possibly. And people like you, Gustaw, if you will? I'll get Rosen posted to the same squadron, if that helps?"

"And Witold Nowacki?"

"Yes, why not? Anyone else? You can handpick a bloody squadron of your Polish friends if you like."

CHAPTER 16

"Tell me why you're so unhappy, Tunio," said Staś, as they moved slowly through the Lancashire mill towns, counting the tall, redbrick chimneys. He, Gus and Nowacki were on a train to their new posting in Southport.

"You've been moved from bombers to fighters and you've got a DFC — why are you so miserable?" added Gus.

"I'm not miserable, am I?" Nowacki protested.

"Yes, you bloody well are," said Gus.

"If I'm honest, I didn't want the medal. I could have died on the wing of that lumbering cart of an aeroplane, yes. But I didn't do it for a British medal. Sorry, Bouncer. A Polish Cross of Valour — now that would be something, but a poxy British Distinguished Flying Cross? No! Sorry again, Bouncer."

"You never told us the full story."

"Didn't I?

"You know you didn't. Come on, tell us everything."

"Then listen. Staś, do you remember when we and the other Dęblin cadets stood there listening to bloody Air Chief Marshal Dowding?" Nowacki began.

"I remember. Eastchurch. Most of us were wearing French Air Force uniforms, our berets at jaunty angles. I could see the Air Chief Marshal wasn't impressed."

"Stuffy," said Gus.

"What?"

"Air Chief Marshal Dowding is called Stuffy. Well, not to his face."

"Stuffy, then. He addressed us through an interpreter. Urged us to be patient. Tried to convince us that first we must learn

English and the ways of the RAF. Flying action would need to wait."

"That's right. But the last thing we wanted was to be was patient," said Staś. "Once he'd finished speaking, Stuffy invited questions. Tunio was up on his feet in an instant."

Nowacki nodded. "'When will we start flying?' I asked him, and the interpreter translated."

"'That depends on a number of circumstances,'" quoted Staś, attempting to imitate the Air Marshal.

"I continued to push him," said Nowacki. "'Well, when will Polish fighter pilots begin their training?' I asked. Remember his answer, Staś?" said Nowacki.

"He told us the first to receive training would be the Polish bomber crews."

"That's right. A couple of weeks later, I learned that I'd been relegated to Bomber Command," said Nowacki. "Lots of us were. We were disappointed because we were fighter pilots, but at least we'd get into action first."

"You phoned me," said Staś. "You were livid. You called the RAF bastards and reminded me of your entire CV — combat instructor at Dęblin, fought 109s and 110s over Poland."

"But I said that if I had to fly slow, unwieldy bombers to get back into this war, I would bloody well do it! But I didn't know why we were posted to the RAF Volunteer Reserve. I asked Staś what it meant."

"What did you tell him?" asked Gus, turning to Staś.

"I told him what you told me. It means we're the new money trying our damned hardest to be officers and gentlemen."

"I didn't understand then and I don't understand now. Of course, we're both officers and gentlemen already," said Nowacki. "But anyway, I did the training on bomber aircraft. I hated it. It's like driving a bus. I was also demoted to Pilot

Officer; all the Polish officers were. Only after retraining and posting would anyone be promoted to a higher rank. The early days were taken up mainly with English lessons, parade ground drills and RAF regulations. Eventually, I was posted to a squadron in southern England flying Vickers Wellingtons, twin-engine bombers. You British call them Wimpys.

"My first action was the first night-bombing raid launched on Berlin. On the way back, somewhere over the Dutch coast, we were attacked by a Messerschmitt 110. We took hits from cannon-shells and incendiary bullets. The rear gunner was wounded, but not before he had managed to let off a burst of fire. That forced the enemy fighter away. Then somebody shouted, 'Smoke from the port engine, Skipper!' It was Jimmy Fowler, yelling from the observer's hatch. I looked out to the left, over the wing. Sure enough, a fire had started. Petrol from a split pipe was spurting onto the flames. The fire was quickly gaining hold and threatened to spread to the entire wing. I ordered Jimmy to take over the controls. He was also the second pilot. 'What are you going to do, Skipper?' he asked. I told him I was going to put out that bloody fire, of course. I instructed Jimmy to keep the speed as low as possible. With the wireless operator and forward gunner, a hammer and some pincers, we forced a hole in the fuselage and tried to reduce the fire using extinguishers. It didn't work. Too much wind from our airspeed — it blew water everywhere."

"Blimey," said Gus. "What did you do next?"

"I told the others to get ready to bail out of the aircraft, but I didn't want to lose the plane. I picked up an engine cover which Walter, the wireless operator, had been using as a cushion. I tied myself to the Wellington with a rope from the dinghy. The crew stared at me; one asked what I was doing. 'I'm going out onto the wing,' I said. They told me to put on a parachute, but I refused at first, because I thought it would cause too much drag. But Walter pleaded with me, so in the end I agreed. We got Jimmy to slow down to just above stall speed.

"With the help of Walter, I climbed through the hole in the port side of the fuselage and onto the wing itself. Jimmy had slowed the Wimpy all he could, but the wind pressure made it very difficult. I could feel myself being buffeted and thought that at any moment I'd be ripped off the wing. It was lucky it was a Wellington."

"Why's that?" asked Gus.

"The Wimpy's wings, like its fuselage, are constructed from a durable aluminium framework and linen fabric is stretched over it. The fabric was doped, causing it to dry drumskin-taut, but it was on the fragile side. I went out onto the port wing, punching and kicking at the fabric to break it and make hand and footholds. With these I could grip and secure myself. And that's how I made my way to the engine. It was slow; my hands were sore and bleeding, my face stung in the ice-cold wind and I was shaking with fear."

"Tunio Nowacki, afraid? I don't believe it," said Staś.

"I tell you, I was shaking. My God, I never want to do anything like that again. But after repeated attempts, I was able to smother the flames with the engine cover. Holding on with one hand, I tried to push the engine cover into the hole in the wing and onto the leaking pipe, but as soon as I let go a terrific wind blew the cover away. I could see that there was now no fabric left near the petrol pipe and so no danger of fire spreading. I made my way back into the Wimpy and almost collapsed. I ordered Jimmy to check our course and increase speed. I said I needed a rest, but I'd come up in half an hour and take over before we descended onto a landing run."

"You needed a rest? You really told him that?" laughed Gus.

"Of course, I bloody well needed a rest. I could have died out there, and for what? For a poxy British Distinguished Flying Cross."

"And that's why you're miserable?"

"No."

"Then why? What the bloody hell is wrong with you?" asked Gus, agitated.

"I'm happy to be going to a Hurricane squadron, but…"

"I'm not," said Staś. "Give me a Spitfire any day."

"Have you flown a Hurricane?" asked Gus.

"Actually, no I haven't."

"Then shut up, Staś. Let's hear what's bothering Tunio so much."

"It's this." He pointed to the single, wide braid on his sleeve. "I was a bloody captain in the Polish Air Force, and I should be a bloody flight lieutenant now! Not a poxy flying officer. That's what it's all about. I should have double braids. Poxy British bloody ranks! Sorry, Bouncer."

Gus and Staś couldn't help themselves; they were creased with laughter by now.

"I wonder who the new squadron leader is?" said Staś, trying to change the subject.

"What? You two don't know?" said Nowacki.

"And you do?" asked Gus.

"That's what comes with being a poxy flying officer," said Staś. "You get all the news first."

"He's a Canadian Auxiliary. Squadron Leader Gordon Johnson — known as Grumpy."

"What's 'grumpy'?" asked Staś.

"Somebody who is usually bad-tempered," explained Gus. "But Squadron Leader Johnson is probably nicknamed

Grumpy because of his light-hearted approach to life. That's the RAF all over."

There were twenty-two pilots at Southport — eighteen Poles, three Czechs and a Latvian — together with over a hundred ground crew. Many of them were still sporting French Air Force uniforms. Talking to them, Gus heard many different tales of escape from the debacle in Poland last year. Some had followed much the same route as Staś and Nowacki. Others had moved through Slovakia to Hungary, then northwards to Lithuania or Latvia. One senior NCO had travelled through the Black Sea and Mediterranean to Egypt and then to England. Gus found them all good airmen — skilled, experienced and ready to fight. *This could turn out to be one of the best fighter squadrons in the RAF*, he thought, *apart from its one big problem: Grumpy Johnson.*

Gus had been wrong about Squadron Leader Johnson. His CO hadn't been nicknamed Grumpy because he was light-hearted, far from it. He was pedantic, bombastic and seemingly determined to wage a personal vendetta against Gus.

At Southport, all they did was drill, acquire some basic English, and learn the outdated RAF tactics that Staś had railed against. The first argument was, perhaps not surprisingly, about the harmonisation of the machine guns. Gus was caught in the middle of a disagreement between Johnson and the Polish pilots.

Like most of the Poles, Nowacki spoke very little English. Staś, on the other hand, was fluent, but he refused to speak English to Johnson. This meant a lot of work for Gus.

"Tell him the problem with the RAF is that the British pilots shoot too early," said Staś. "Tell him we will close the distance down to two hundred metres and we want the guns harmonised at that range."

"Agreed," said Nowacki.

"What are they saying, Beaumont?"

"Pilot Officer Rosen politely requests that the guns are harmonised at two hundred yards, sir. Flying Officer Nowacki supports him."

"Bollocks!" said Staś. "I've no intention of being polite to him."

"You can speak for yourself, then," said Gus.

"What was that, Beaumont?" Johnson interrupted.

"Pilot Officer Rosen says two hundred and fifty yards will be acceptable."

"No, I don't!"

"Yes, you do, Staś. The guns on Hurricanes are closer together than the Spitfires. You won't need to get as close as you did in a bloody P-11; it only had two guns anyway."

"The regulations are crystal clear," said Johnson. "They stipulate that we are to harmonise the machine guns at six hundred yards so as to create a 'Dowding spread' of fire into an eight by twelve-foot rectangle. This makes it more likely that a mediocre fighter pilot will score a hit."

"Who's he calling mediocre?" blurted Staś, angrily.

"What did he say, Beaumont?" Johnson snapped.

"Nothing important, sir." And so it went on.

The next day Gus was summoned into Squadron Leader Johnson's office. He stood to attention and saluted.

"At ease, Beaumont. I've some news, and I want you to relate it to the Polish men."

"Yes, sir."

"The squadron is moving from Southport to London the day after tomorrow. And we will begin flying Hurricanes."

"Yes, sir," beamed Gus, delighted that he would be moving closer to Eunice. He decided to write to her straight away, asking her to meet him in the tearoom on Greek Street.

A few days later, the Polish squadron had settled into their new base and Gus was waiting for Eunice in their usual tearoom. Eventually the door flew open and in she swept. Flustered and angry, Eunice sat down and spat at him, "Be honest with me, Gus, does my tummy need holding in? Does it?"

Gus smiled. "No, Eunice, your tummy is as flat as a pancake. It definitely doesn't need holding in; it looks lovely. Why do you ask?"

"Because at today's shoot they made me model a bloody girdle," she explained, outraged.

"A girdle?" he laughed.

"Not just any girdle. A brand-new Living Girdle manufactured in the States by the International Latex Corporation. Ronnie, he was the shoot director, told me that it's being marketed as indestructible, resistant to holes and snags. So he said he needed some good shots of me dancing and cavorting around with a lovely smile on my face to show how comfortable the thing is. Bloody cheek."

"What did you say?"

"I told him that if he wanted me to smile, he'd need to turn the bloody electric fire on. It was freezing in there. He just glanced at the two-bar heater and pointed out that it was July and they couldn't afford it. I asked if he had any music, but he hadn't thought of that. Instead, he offered to sing while the photographer, Ben, took the snaps. Ronnie sang 'Roll out the Barrel' then hummed Glenn Miller's 'Little Brown Jug'. Meanwhile, I was dressed in the ILC Living Girdle, a bra with pointed cups and a pair of black nylons. I danced as best I could, and Ben took the photographs. After the shoot I kept the nylons on, dressed in my own clothes, picked up my gasmask case and rushed down the hill to Brixton, and here I am. All yours."

Gus looked at her wistfully. German bombers had begun their attacks on Britain and the brave young pilots of the RAF were scrambling daily, taking to the air to meet them. In London the air-raid sirens wailed night and day and people were beginning to panic, donning their gasmasks just in case. Britain was at war, and Eunice Hesketh's contribution was in a cold and dingy Streatham studio, posing in underwear and stockings.

"Why do you keep on with it?" he asked.

"Peacock insists that I carry on with the photographic modelling. He said it would be an excellent cover. Henry Pillinger has relocated to America, where the fashion industry is carrying on regardless. He tipped me off to some work with an outfit called Destiny, which is based here but sending images to New York for publication. The pay's awful, but at least I got to keep the nylons today. What about you?"

"Well, as you know, my squadron has been moved to London, Northolt and…"

"Northolt? That's hardly London — it's miles away," Eunice laughed.

"It's a darned sight nearer than Southport, or even West Malling. I was pleased and thought you would be, too. I thought we might see a little more of each other, actually."

"That would be nice," she said. Eunice smiled and held out her hand. As Gus took it in his, he thought he might be falling in love with her. Again.

CHAPTER 17

"When are you going to let us loose on those damned Nazis?" asked Tunio Nowacki, aggressively.

Two weeks had gone by since the squadron's relocation to Northolt, and still they hadn't been approved to start flying missions. Exasperated with the situation, Tunio and Staś had gone to see Squadron Leader Johnson in his office, dragging a reluctant Gus along to translate.

"Look," answered Johnson, "tell the bugger his men have got to get the basics right first. 303 Squadron are just as bad. They had a Hurricane badly damaged in a landing incident two days ago. Does he know that?"

"He was an experienced pilot and a first-class flyer, better than any of you British flyers," said Nowacki. "He simply forgot to lower the undercarriage before touching down."

"What did he say, Beaumont?"

"Flying Officer Nowacki explained that he is aware of that, sir."

"It's because he couldn't understand the control tower warning him. The bloody Poles must learn enough English to be able to communicate over their radios," said Johnson. "The group leader will not, I repeat, will not, under any circumstances make the squadron operational without being convinced the Poles can complete missions safely. He thinks there will be mayhem in the air."

"There needs to be bloody mayhem," said Nowacki, "mayhem against the bastard Nazis."

"He says he will make learning English a priority for all the Polish pilots, sir," lied Gus.

Over the next two weeks Gus and Staś, assisted by two other pilots who spoke English, made enormous efforts to teach the Poles the basics of the language they would need in order to communicate with other RAF units and ground control. They did a good job and, once the Poles had become convinced it was a necessity, they focused on their studies and made rapid progress.

"Time to relax," said Nowacki, after an intensive set of lessons.

"Relax? There's a bloody war on, or had you forgotten?"

"A man has to wind down sometime. Me and Staś met two young ladies a few weeks ago. We're seeing them again tonight."

"You did? You didn't say anything."

"Well, there's nothing to say really," said Staś.

"Staś and I went into a pub in Uxbridge. It was packed full of British airmen, WAAFs and some civilians. People were dancing to music. It was funny. There was an elderly woman playing a piano, which was slightly out of tune. Anyway, everyone seemed to be having a good time. We felt uncomfortable at first, I suppose. After a few beers we joined in the fun. Staś pointed out two women looking at us. They sat together, sipping half pint drinks. One was a civilian and the other a WAAF. I told Staś the one in uniform looked very nice. So Staś said he'd ask the one in civvies for a dance, and I could dance with the WAAF."

"Sounds easy," said Gus.

"It was," said Staś. "They were keen to dance."

"We didn't stop until the piano player needed a toilet break. Staś sat us down and went to get more drinks. The young woman in WAAF uniform asked our names, so I told her. Then she and her friend introduced themselves: the woman in civvies was Avis and the WAAF was Milly. I said I was pleased to meet them, and we really hit it off from then on."

"And how is it going?"

"Fine," said Nowacki, "just fine. Milly is really nice. I'd like her to meet you. You and your girl, Bouncer."

"That would be nice. Maybe you would like to join Eunice and me one evening. It could be fun if we all go out together. What do you think?"

"It won't work," said Staś.

"Why won't it work?"

"They're working class, and we're not. And Eunice is a — what is it, Bouncer? A toff?"

"Nonsense," said Gus. "Eunice isn't a toff. She's as down-to-earth as they get."

"You'll see," said Staś.

"We can all go," said Nowacki. "You can bring Avis."

"No. I'm not seeing her again. My choice, not hers."

"Because she's working class?" suggested Gus. "You're a bloody snob."

Staś scowled.

"Friday night then, Tunio," said Gus. "Assuming nothing blows up too badly between now and then."

"We're just training. You know that. Nothing will bloody well blow up."

As Nowacki spoke, the door flew open and an airman rushed in.

"I've just had a phone call from Urbanowicz at 303," he said excitedly. "They're to be mobilised tomorrow."

"Great news! What happened?" asked Nowacki.

"They were up today, still training. One of the men thought he'd spotted a Dornier and broke off from the rest to attack it. Turned out it was a Messerschmitt 110, but he still shot it down. Stuffy got the news and decided to mobilise the squadron."

"If 303 can be operational, then so can we. We're easily as good. Let's go and see Grumpy, now," said Nowacki. "Come on, Bouncer. You too, Staś."

They sped to Squadron HQ and demanded to see Johnson. In his office, they stood to attention and saluted.

"What is it now, Beaumont?" asked the squadron leader.

"The Poles have learned that 303 Squadron is to become operational, sir. They request that your squadron becomes operational too and that you contact Air Marshal Dowding to that effect, sir."

"No! There's no bloody way these damned foreigners are fit to fight, Beaumont. The Poles are poor pilots. They lasted just three days against the Luftwaffe last year and I have no reason to suppose that they would do any better operating from England. Tell them that."

"He doesn't need to tell me anything," said Staś. "I understand you perfectly, Squadron Leader Johnson. I wish to tender my resignation, as I have no confidence in your leadership of this squadron." Staś turned to Nowacki and spoke to him briefly in Polish.

"I am with Pilot Officer Rosen," said Nowacki.

Johnson rounded on Gus. "Is this your doing, Beaumont? Have you been winding up the buggers?"

"That isn't fair, sir."

"Not fair? I'll have you up for insubordination, young man. Now, get out of my office, all of you."

"It worked," said Gus with a grin as the three of them sauntered back to the mess, "you called Grumpy's bluff."

"I knew he wouldn't accept our resignations," said a gleeful Staś. "The RAF needs pilots. We'll be operational within a week. Mark my words."

CHAPTER 18

Two days later, the men were still awaiting the consequences of their confrontation with Johnson. However, Gus tried to put it out of his mind as he and Nowacki made their way to the local pub for their date with Eunice and Milly.

They arrived in good time and the two young women arrived shortly after. Gus began the introductions.

"This is Eunice Hesketh," he said. "Eunice, I'd like you to meet my friend, Flying Officer Witold Nowacki."

"Pleased to meet you," said Eunice as they shook hands.

"My friends call me Tunio. I'd like you both to meet my friend, Miss Millicent Turner."

"Pleased to meet you. Please call me Milly."

"I'll get us some drinks. What would you like?" asked Gus.

"A Kir Royale," said Eunice.

"You'll be lucky," said Gus. "There's no bloody French fizz. There's a war on, you know. Milly?"

"A milk stout, please."

"Pint of bitter for me," said Nowacki.

Gus went to order the drinks. Snippets of the conversation at the table reached him.

"You're not from around here, are you, Milly?" asked Eunice.

"No. I'm from Salford. It's part of Manchester."

"When did you come here?"

"Just before the war."

"What did you do in Salford, before the war?"

"I worked in the UCP café."

"UCP? What's that?"

"What? You've never heard of it? It stands for Universal Cattle Products. Funny, because they sell pigs' trotters as well as tripe in the shop. But it's the best café in town!"

"Well, it must be a northern thing, that's all I can say. We don't have them up here in London."

"Down here, you mean."

"What?"

"It's up north and down south."

"No, no, Milly it's up in London. Always up."

Gus returned with the drinks. Two pints of beer, a milk stout for Milly and a schooner full of pinkish liquid.

"I asked for a Kir Royale and the barman looked at me quizzically. He'd obviously never heard of it."

Eunice took a sip. "What is it?"

"White port with blackcurrant."

"It's rather nice. A bit sweet, maybe."

"What do you do, Eunice?" asked Milly.

"Oh, nothing much. I model clothes for fashion magazines."

Milly almost choked on her milk stout. "You do what?"

"I know it sounds glamourous, but…"

"I just love clothes," said Milly. "Could you show me some of the photos?"

"Yes. I'll bring some next time. But it's not important work. I feel useless, to be honest!"

"I used to feel like that when I first came down, I mean up, here. You see, just before the war, I gave up my job at the UCP in Manchester and got on the train to London. I was to spend the summer looking after my auntie in Cowley. Auntie Edna, that is. She's my dad's cousin, so not my aunt at all. Edna was a lot younger than my dad, but she'd lost a leg to gangrene and when Alan, that's her husband, was killed in an industrial accident, Edna simply couldn't cope with their three children. Cowley isn't much different to Salford, but Edna's pension from the brickworks kept us pretty well off. Edna gave me spending money, so on Friday and Saturday nights, once the kids were in bed, I'd walk or catch a bus to Uxbridge then get the Metropolitan line into town. I'd go to a dance hall, maybe the Hammersmith Palais, sometimes one of the smaller ones." Milly paused and took a sip of her stout.

"Anyway, all of a sudden war with Germany was declared. A couple of days later I walked the children, Thomas, Sydney and little Ellen, to West Drayton station. They were to be evacuated."

"It's best to get children out of the cities and into the countryside, where they'll be safe. I expect they'll have a whale of a time."

"How can the government expect young children to settle with unknown families in unknown places, thinking all the time that their parents are being bombed to death by the Germans?" asked Eunice.

"That's right," said Milly. "My younger sister, Bertha, was evacuated to Blackpool during the Czech crisis. She couldn't sleep and spent most of the time crying. Eventually, our mam had to go to Blackpool and bring her home."

"I hadn't thought of that," said Gus. "It must be hard."

"The poor little so and so's," said Milly. "Each of them carried a small case of belongings. Ellen and Syd were tearful, but Thomas seemed to grow up overnight. He looked like he was bearing up well enough."

"Did they get off all right?"

"No. As we waited for the train, there was Edna hobbling awkwardly along the platform on her one leg, helped by her neighbour, Mrs McGregor. She said she just couldn't let them walk off like that — she had to see them off herself. Well, life caught up with young Thomas, who burst into tears. That started the other two wailing again. Just as I thought the situation couldn't possibly get any worse, Edna collapsed. Then the train arrived."

"Bloody hell. What a story," said Eunice.

"As Mrs McGregor and Thomas helped Edna up, the train screeched to a standstill. Scores of children, most of them in tears, began to clamber on board. Sydney was brave and climbed into a carriage. I pulled Thomas away from his mother and shoved him and his sister onto the train. Then the train pulled out of West Drayton and left the lot of us crying on the platform."

"Who's for another drink?" asked Gus. "Same again?"

"Can I have the same as Eunice, please?" said Milly.

Gus went to the bar to get more drinks, keeping one ear tuned in to the conversation.

"Aunt Edna didn't need me so much after the kids had gone, and I started going out dancing more," continued Milly. "At first, I was worried about going alone. I don't think I'd have done it up north. But here in London, things seem somehow freer. I met a girl called Avis who lived in Ickenham, and soon we were going to dances together. We'd dance together, dance with young men, chat about the men we danced with, then dance some more. It was all innocent fun and I loved it. One Saturday night we sat in a pub, here in Uxbridge, smoking and chatting, when a group of young women came in. They wore smart, blue-grey uniforms with Royal Air Force insignia. I asked Avis who they were, and she said they were WAAFs from the Uxbridge RAF base. Avis didn't know exactly what they did, but it was something to do with plotting German aircraft on big maps. I decided then and there that that was what I was going to do: join the WAAFs and do something in this bloody war."

"And you did," said Eunice. "Good for you, Milly."

"I was sent to Wilmslow for training."

"What was it like?"

"At first it was mostly physical training, which we did every day inside a large gymnasium. I hated the PT kit," Milly said, frowning. "Plimsols, socks that came to just below the knee, a horrible skirt that ended just above the knee and a tight-fitting, short-sleeved shirt that our bras showed though."

"Oh my God, how dreadful."

"Everything was dark grey. General training included gasmask drill, first aid, self-defence and unarmed combat — I really enjoyed that…"

"Don't mess with this young lady, Tunio," joked Gus as he returned with the second round of drinks.

"And there was marching — endless drilling and marching. But do you know what? I never saw an aeroplane. Not once!" Milly paused and took a sip of her white port with blackcurrant. She lit a cigarette. "Once I'd completed basic training, I became Aircraft Woman Second Class Turner WAAF. I was so proud. My blue-grey uniform wasn't altogether fetching…"

"Oh, I think it is," said Nowacki.

"What? A calf-length skirt and heavy, woollen stockings?"

"The tunic's smart, though," said Eunice. "That tight belt high around your middle shows off your slim waist. It does look nice, Milly. Can I try it on, sometime? We're about the same size, and I quite like the thought of wearing a necktie. And the hat finishes the uniform off jauntily, doesn't it, Gus?"

"What did you do after qualifying, Milly?" asked Gus, blushing slightly and trying to change the subject.

"The girls went off in different directions and to different specialisms. Some went to parachute-packing, others to crewing barrage balloons, performing catering, meteorology, radar, aircraft maintenance, transport, and wireless telephonic and telegraphic operation. Some worked with codes and ciphers, analysing reconnaissance photographs. My job was to be a plotter in an operation room, which they told me was a vital role in the control of aircraft."

"It is, we can assure you," said Gus, and Nowacki nodded.

"I'm based here at RAF Uxbridge, as you know. Part of 11 Group, Fighter Command. I really couldn't be happier."

CHAPTER 19

It was exactly a week following the men's argument with Johnson. News had arrived, but Johnson didn't share it with the pilots himself. He left it to his adjutant.

"Orders have come through from 11 Group," the adjutant announced, "that the Polish squadrons are to be operational. Gentlemen, you'll all no doubt be pleased to learn that you will fly in anger from tomorrow."

The Poles cheered. Gus wondered whether Johnson had been overruled on Peacock's say-so, or whether Stuffy Dowding had decided he just needed every fighter pilot available. It didn't matter. The Poles were elated.

"So why are we waiting?" asked Staś.

"You know the system," answered Gus. "Radar and ground observation will locate targets for us. It's no use us being up there, burning fuel. Just be patient."

"Milly is down in that bunker now," said Nowacki. "She'll find targets for us, just you see. Then we'll scramble and shoot the bastards down. After, we're going out to celebrate."

"How can we celebrate while knowing what's happening in Poland?" asked Staś.

"Whatever we do or don't do, it won't change anything there," said Nowacki, "so we're going out, and you're coming too. You don't have a young lady, so maybe get one here. You could be dead next week."

"Thanks, Tunio! But I don't want to."

"Are you jealous because Gus and I have girls and you don't?"

"Jealous?" asked Staś.

"Yes. You could try harder with Milly's friend, Avis. She's not so bad."

Thoroughly riled, Staś squared up to Nowacki, who took a step towards him. Gus quickly got between the two Poles. "Calm down, both of you!" he shouted, and as he did, the alarm sounded. It was time to scramble.

A flight of Hurricanes was in the air within minutes. Johnson led Yellow section and Nowacki led Red. They closed together and headed on the bearing provided by ground control. The Poles' first move was to gain more height, then position their attack so as to attack out of the sun, where it was most difficult for the German pilots to spot them. Having done so, Nowacki was first to spot a clutch of Heinkels escorted by six Messerschmitt Bf-109s. He radioed this to Johnson. "Enemy at three o'clock, Angels ten."

"Roger that; I'll lead Yellow to attack the bombers," said Johnson. "Nowacki, you are to take Red section and disrupt those 109s."

Before he had finished giving his orders, Nowacki had pointed to the German fighters and peeled off towards them. "Tally-ho!" he shouted into the RT.

The Poles swept down onto the unsuspecting 109s. Nowacki's Hurricane was the lead fighter, the first to dive with the bright sun behind him. He closed in and opened fire, shooting down his chosen target with a stinging volley of .303 hail. Staś selected his target and dived towards it. Gaining on the 109, faithful to his theory that the RAF pilots opened fire too soon, Staś closed to an almost unimaginable point-blank range before opening fire. He pushed the button on his control column and the eight Browning guns spat fire at the 109. The German plane was decimated by the close-range firepower of the Hurricane, disappearing from the sky in an explosion of flames and smoke.

As those leading Hurricanes opened fire, the Messerschmitts broke formation. Then it was every pilot for himself as the rival fighters banked, turned, climbed and dived for advantage. There was almost no way the RAF's wingman system could manage. Quickly, as the Germans dispersed, Nowacki followed a second Messerschmitt fighter. He closed on the German, fixing it in his gun sights, but it seemed he was out of ammunition. Rather than turning back to base, Nowacki closed the distance and climbed right above the 109. The German pilot must have been so shocked to see the underside of a Hurricane within arm's reach of his cockpit that he instinctively reduced his altitude to avoid a collision. He lost control and his Messerschmitt crashed into the ground, bursting into flames on impact.

Gus, meanwhile, was being tailed by a Messerschmitt Bf-109. He pulled back on the stick as hard as he possibly could. The Merlin engine was screaming as he put the Hurricane into a vertical climb, the first part of a loop the loop. As the fighter turned upside-down, Gus rolled her over and entered the dive, facing the Messerschmitt. It was now five hundred feet below him, heading east. The German pilot had clearly given up; maybe he was low on petrol or out of ammunition.

Gus checked his own fuel level; he knew he had plenty of ammunition for the Browning guns. He turned to pursue the 109, which began to weave a frantic, zigzag course. *He's trying to throw me off*, he thought. *Well, he can think again.*

With height advantage, Gus came closer and closer to the German. In a dive, he found he could outpace the 109 and was gaining on it. Gus had the Messerschmitt in his sights. As the German swerved and twisted at sea level, Gus stuck to it like glue. Strong glue at that. He was awaiting his opportunity for a good, long burst from the .303 Browning machine guns. Eventually it came, and he fired at the Messerschmitt's tail. No smoke. No glycol, but Gus was sure he'd scored a hit.

Whether it was tiredness or injury on the Nazi's part, Gus would never know, but the German pilot made a mistake. Again, he turned to the left, but this time his turn was too shallow. It gave Gus a chance to shoot at the port side of the Messerschmitt. He pressed the fire button on the stick. The Hurricane shook violently as the guns and cannons discharged all the remaining ammo into the German fighter. Smoke and glycol poured off the Messerschmitt's engine, and the pilot bailed out.

It was his first kill. Since opening fire on those German soldiers back in May, in that futile Lysander attack, Gus hadn't fired in anger until now. He was pleased to have downed one Messerschmitt and shifted off another, but also quietly pleased that the German pilot had made it safely out of the burning aeroplane. Gus had no desire to take a life for the sake of it. It was enough to put a 109 and its pilot out of the war.

Eventually, the Poles returned to base and handed in their combat reports. Johnson's Yellow section had downed three Heinkels with two probable kills in addition, whilst Red had four Bf-109s for certain and another probable.

"I'm going to see Milly," said Nowacki that evening. "We're meeting in Uxbridge after her shift. I don't think I'll be back in the mess tonight. Cover for me?"

"And I'm off to see Eunice," added Gus. "You'll need to cover for both of us, Staś. Are you all right with that?"

"I am — it'll be fine. You two go and enjoy yourselves. Don't worry about me," said Staś.

Gus and Nowacki left the base together but parted ways soon after; while Nowacki was travelling to Uxbridge, Gus was heading towards central London. He met up with Eunice in a quiet pub and found a table.

"I asked Milly to tell me what it is like in that underground bunker," said Eunice once they were settled. "I wanted to know all about it — if it's damp and dingy, for example. Milly told me it's brand new and has air conditioning. It's a bit cold, though. I wanted to know exactly what she does down there. She told me that about twenty WAAFs work around a big table that has a huge map of southern England on it. They have headphones and when they're told of a sighting of enemy planes, bombers or fighters, they place them onto the map in the correct positions. They use big, long sticks to move them around. Other girls are in charge of charting the position of our squadrons; when an RAF squadron is scrambled, it's positioned onto the same map. Around the walls are charts showing the status of each RAF squadron, whether it's ready to go, airborne, or back refuelling. Overlooking all of them is the Command Room, and the officers in there are taking everything in and deciding what to do next."

"I'm not sure Milly should have told you all of that. Careless talk costs lives and all that."

"Oh, don't be such a fuddy-duddy, Gus. She's making a contribution to this bloody war. Not like me. I told Milly I envied her. She's doing something valuable. I should be, too. She said I could volunteer to join the WAAFs."

"She's right, you could. But somehow, I don't think it's quite you," said Gus.

"She said being a WAAF wasn't glamourous like modelling clothes, and she'd swap with me any day to do some modelling. So I told her she can come with me to give modelling a try."

"You didn't! What did she say?"

"She was surprised, but I told her she certainly has the figure for it. Milly does have a nice figure, doesn't she, Gus?" said Eunice, a cheeky smile on her face.

"Actually, I don't go around looking at my pal's girl in that sort of way."

"Don't believe you," said Eunice.

CHAPTER 20

That summer, every day was the same for the Polish squadron. The alarms would sound and the Poles would scramble, fighting fiercely in the blue skies of their adopted country. After the dogfights, the pilots would sit, smoke, eat, recover, and sometimes discuss tactics.

Today, a scramble had been called for the third time. Eight Polish pilots sprinted to the Hurricanes, which were parked in sandbag-protected bays. Engines roared to life, and the aircraft taxied in unison towards the runway, took off and were soon directed towards an incoming formation of Junkers Ju-88 bombers.

As the Hurricanes climbed to gain the all-important height advantage over their slower foes, Staś spotted a clutch of enemy fighters above them. "Bogies, eight o'clock, ten thousand feet," he radioed.

Gus listened and looked for the enemy fighters. He saw the Bf-110s, but it was too late. Messerschmitt fighters were diving towards them even as Staś spoke over the radio.

"Break, break!" shouted Johnson. The Hurricanes scattered into four pairs, desperately trying to avoid the 110s, but severely hampered by the superior dive speed of the German aircraft.

The flight was decimated. Gus watched in horror as the 110s, with their black crosses, swastikas, and yellow-painted noses with shark's teeth, dived and opened fire. Flying Officer Szwed was killed when his Hurricane was hit by cannon fire and exploded. Flight Sergeant Marek crashed into the ground after being wounded. Johnson, his Hurricane badly damaged and out of control, bailed out and was wounded on landing. Staś had to make a forced landing with a damaged undercarriage and was slightly wounded. Flight Sergeant Jankowski was severely burned when his aircraft burst into flames upon landing. The others got back, but they were badly beaten up and demoralised. Two pilots killed, two badly wounded and another slightly. Four aircraft lost, a further four damaged.

There was just one spot of good news for the courageous Poles. The following day, Nowacki was promoted to flight lieutenant and given acting leadership of the squadron.

"Yes," he said, "you can call me Squadron Leader Nowacki for now!"

The Poles cheered him.

Later, Nowacki came to see Gus in the bar at the mess.

"I've been thinking," he said. "If we're bounced by German fighters, simply scattering the way Grumpy ordered yesterday is no use. We're easy meat for the Nazis that way."

"What do you suggest?"

Nowacki took a notebook and pencil and drew a diagram of two aeroplanes. One he labelled 'A', the other 'B'. Then he drew the flight paths of these two imaginary fighters. They formed a weaving pattern, 'A' going left-right-left while 'B' flew right-left-right, meaning their courses intersected at regular intervals.

"Look," said Nowacki, "I'm flying fighter 'A' and you're my wingman in fighter 'B'. We start off side by side, then fly like this —" he pointed to the diagram — "turning towards each other in fairly tight weaves. After crossing paths, and once our separation is big enough, we repeat the exercise, again turning in towards each other. The Luftwaffe pilot has to tail one of us to engage in battle. And he will have to decide quickly; he can't stay looking around for long because his fuel is limited. When the enemy chooses one of us as his target, that one becomes the bait."

Gus considered this and concluded that Nowacki was correct. Any Messerschmitt pilot in that situation would choose one or the other, probably the closest.

"Let's say I'm the bait. I simply keep up the same pattern of weave. The Messerschmitt has to slow down a little now, or I go out of his sights, so it doesn't matter that he's a little bit faster. Agree?"

"Yes," said Gus. "Carry on."

"Now you, my wingman, are behind both of us. As I weave, I come in front of you. And so does he, and when he does…"

"When he does, I blast the bastard out of the sky!" said Gus.

"I think it will work. And, what's more, it could also be used by four of us, flying side by side in two pairs, the two wingmen bringing the enemy plane into their sights. Assuming the bait is taken, a correctly executed weave leaves little chance of escape for even the fastest and most manoeuvrable opponent."

"You're a genius, Tunio. A bloody marvel!" said Gus.

"There's something else," said Nowacki. "Something personal."

"About Milly?"

"Yes."

"She's not finished with you, has she?"

"No, not that."

"She and Eunice seem to have foxed Staś's bloody silly idea that class differences would create an unsurmountable divide between them," said Gus.

"I think he's sorry," said Nowacki. "Milly and Eunice seem to have hit it off all right."

"I'd say so. They're friends," said Gus.

"I hope it lasts," said Nowacki, "because..."

There was a sound at the door and Staś burst in.

"Hello, Staś," said Gus. "Have you noticed that you're now estimating altitude in feet, not metres? I thought something sounded odd over the RT."

"Never mind that!" shouted Staś. "Those Bf-110s that bounced us earlier — it was the same squadron that we fought in Poland. Tunio, remember the colour scheme?"

"Yes, you're right," said Nowacki. "Yellow noses with shark's teeth, picked out in white on red."

"I'm sure it was them," said Staś. "They were the butchers that killed Jan Grudziński."

CHAPTER 21

Replacement Hurricanes arrived within a couple of days. The first was delivered by a female pilot of the Air Transport Auxiliary. The Poles watched as the new Hurricane landed perfectly on the grassy strip and taxied over to the hangars.

As the short and slightly plump young woman climbed out of the cockpit, she removed her flying helmet to reveal bright red lips and was greeted by a host of wolf-whistling Polish airmen.

"Nice landing, lovely!" shouted out one young officer. "You that good between the bedsheets?"

Like lightning, the woman rounded on him. "Listen, you," she said, "I've flown Spitfires, Hurricanes, Harvards and Wellington bombers, and I've done so without radio or navigation aids. I just used maps, a compass and a watch. So I'm taking no lip from you, neither in the cockpit nor between any sheets. If you give me, or any of the other girls, any more cheek, I'll go straight to your CO and you'll be on a charge! Understand me?"

"Yes, miss," said the Polish flyer, now looking decidedly embarrassed. "I'm so sorry. Look, there's food and drink in the officers' mess if you're hungry." He pointed towards the mess.

"Thanks," she said, glaring at him. "Don't mind if I do, actually."

She jumped down from the Hurricane's wing and off she bounded, in the direction the young Pole had pointed. Gus followed and quickly caught her up.

"Crikey," he said, "that was a proper mauling you gave him, if you don't mind me saying. You were quite right to tell him off, of course, and if you want to, we can see the squadron leader and have him formally reprimanded. I'm the translator, by the way."

"Translator? Are you really? Well, that young man didn't seem to need a translator, did he? No, its fine. I'd much rather leave it. He seemed to calm down, anyway."

"If you're sure?"

"Completely sure. Now, tell me, what does a girl need to do hereabouts to get herself some tucker and a decent cup of tea?"

Gus called for the orderly and ordered two breakfasts and two mugs of tea. "Do take a seat," he said, and the flyer sat down.

"I'm Bernice Kermode," she said, offering her hand. "People call me Bunty."

"I'm Gus Beaumont. Nice to meet you." Gus offered a hand, which Bunty shook fiercely. "My friends call me Bouncer."

"Good to meet you too, Bouncer! Bunty and Bouncy! Hey, we could make a lovely couple, couldn't we? Have you got a lady friend?" When Gus blushed, Bunty laughed at him. "I think you do!" She was still laughing when the food trays arrived.

"Look," said Gus, "can we talk about flying? Were you telling the truth when you told Flying Officer Bartoszyn that you fly without radio or navigation aids and just use maps and a compass?"

"And a watch," said Bunty. "Yes, I always tell the truth, Bouncer darling."

"I'm intrigued. Do tell me more."

"You are such a cutie, aren't you?" said Bunty. "You know, when I told that — what's his name?"

"Flying Officer Bartoszyn."

"Yes. When I told Flying Officer Bartoszyn I'd take no lip from him between any sheets —" she shot Gus a cheeky wink — "it's not because I'm a prude or anything."

Gus felt himself blushing again.

"No need to be bashful, Bouncer," said Bunty. "It's quite normal, you know. Boy meets girl — or, in this case, Bouncy meets Bunty and wham-bam, rantum-scantum!"

"Look, Bunty, the navigation, can you talk me through it? Please?"

"Well, if I must. By the way, are you covering the bill for this lot?" Bunty waved her hand over the food as she asked.

"Yes, of course."

"Then get me another mug of tea, Bouncer. Then I'll talk!" Once Gus had done so, Bunty explained all. "The powers that be don't want to waste time training us on how to use the navigational equipment, you see. We usually plan our own routes, including unmistakeable landmarks — rivers, castles, you know? I always plot the route on a map. The compass and watch can come in handy if I need to do any dead-reckoning. Then we fly low enough so as to be able to see the ground the whole flight long. I picked up that Hurricane at the Gloster works in Hucclecote, flew on a bearing to Oxford, then followed the Thames as far as Windsor. After that, I used the lakes and reservoirs to navigate up to Northolt, and here I am! Simple, really. Tell me, Bouncer, why the interest?"

"I was once caught out when a gyroscopic compass packed up on me," he lied.

"Golly! What did Bouncy boy do?"

"Descended to a low height and looked out for something I could identify. I thought afterwards that I'd like to learn how to do it better. What about poor weather? Low cloud?"

"Bit of a bugger, those, but we cope. I say, Bouncy darling, how about a bacon sarnie? I'm still peckish."

When Bunty had finished eating, she asked for a lift to the closest railway station. "I've got a rail warrant to get me home," she said.

"Where's home?" asked Gus.

"Gloucester. Why? Do you want to come home with me, Bouncy?"

Gus blushed and walked Bunty to the squadron car, where he opened the door of the Humber for her. Once he'd got used to her effusive ways, Gus started to think that this young woman with her larger-than-life personality was actually quite attractive. She was nice and fun to be with, quite unlike Eunice, who, he had begun to realise, often left him downbeat.

"Maybe one day," he said, "but…"

"But now there's a war on, I know!"

When they arrived at West Drayton station, Bunty shoved a piece of paper into his hand and kissed him on the cheek.

"If you ever find yourself in Gloucester and stuck for something to do, look me up," she said. Then she got out of the car and bounded over to the station entrance.

A few days later, four replacement pilots arrived. They came from a mix of backgrounds. Two were Poles from Poland, another was a Pole from the USA who didn't speak Polish, and the last was a Czech, who did.

Nowacki walked up to the four men, Gus and Staś closely behind. He saluted; the officers responded.

"Gentlemen," said Nowacki, "welcome to the best squadron in the RAF and the second best, after the Kościuszko Squadron that is, in the bloody world! On my left is the finest pilot in the squadron, the only one of us to have flown P-11s in Poland, Morane-Saulnier 406s in France, and Spitfires and Hurricanes here — Pilot Officer Staś Rosen." The replacements' eyes widened. "On my left is Pilot Officer Gustaw Beaumont — not the pilot with the softest landing in the squadron, so we call him Bouncer. He's nevertheless an asset; he's our interpreter." Nowacki continued to outline the basics that the new men needed to know. Gus translated for the American's benefit.

"Any questions?" asked Nowacki.

"Sir," said the American, "please may I ask Pilot Officer Rosen, what's the better plane? A Hurricane or a Spitfire?"

"What's your name, son?" asked Nowacki.

"Flying Officer Butch Paderewski Junior, sir. I'm from Krakow — that's Krakow Wisconsin, sir."

"Butch? Nice name. Listen, Butch. We don't stand on ceremony in this squadron, at least not when Squadron Leader Johnson's absent. So, unless the men are around, or I'm reprimanding you, it's Tunio. Pilot Officer Rosen is Staś, and you can call our interpreter Bouncer or Gus. Now, ask again."

"Staś, what's the better plane? A Hurricane or a Spit?" asked Butch Paderewski.

"Good question. First, they're both a damned sight better that a P-11, and they're better than both the Messerschmitt 109 and 110. You'll be glad to know that! Second, they have the same engine, and it's a beauty. The Rolls-Royce Merlin, though it does tend to overheat in the Spit, because of the position of the air intake. On paper, the Spit is faster, six hundred kilometres per hour against the Hurricane's five-fifty."

Paderewski looked at him blankly.

"The Spit has a top speed of three-seventy miles per hour, the Hurricane three-forty," said Gus helpfully.

"But honestly," said Staś, "I can say that despite the Hurricane being slower on paper, I think it's faster than both a Bf-109 or a Spitfire, especially in a dive. The Spit is far more agile and has a tighter turn. The Hurricane is less manoeuvrable than the Spitfire. But the Hurricane handles far better, has a better feel, and is more manoeuvrable than the German fighters. Hand on heart, I prefer the Hurricane."

"Any more questions?" Gus asked the replacement pilots. "No? Well then, I'll tell you why the RAF has more Hurricanes than Spitfires. A new Spit costs twelve thousand six hundred pounds. Any guesses how much a Hurricane costs? No? Well, let me tell you. A new Hurricane costs just four thousand pounds. That's why the RAF prefers them."

CHAPTER 22

Gus sat with Eunice and Milly at a table in the mess. Tunio Nowacki was at the bar, ordering drinks. "Put it on my mess bill," Gus had told him, knowing the Polish officers had next to no money.

"So how did the modelling go?" he asked the two women.

"Lovely," said Milly. "We met up in Streatham. I asked Eunice if she really thought it was going to go all right. You see, when she said I could have a go at some modelling, I didn't think it would really happen and I was nervous."

"I told her she'd need to be calm in the studio. Some girls do get too nervous in front of the camera," said Eunice. "We undressed behind a curtain in one corner of the studio. We're about the same size, Milly and I, so we tried on all of the dresses."

Nowacki came back with the drinks: two pints of pale ale for him and Gus, half a milk stout for Milly and something in a flute for Eunice.

"The barman told me that he can't make you a Kir Royale properly, because he just can't get the fizz," said Nowacki. "This is a Plymouth sloe gin with soda. He hopes it's acceptable."

"Forget the Kir Royale, Tunio," said Eunice. "Your girl looked fantastic in the dresses, especially that blue satin ballgown. It shimmered in the light with every move she made."

"How I wish I could have seen you dressed like that, Milly. But you are always beautiful to me, you know that."

"I was worried that the neckline was a bit too low," said Milly.

"Nonsense. Nothing wrong with flashing a little bit of bust, Mills. It'll wake up the men," said Eunice.

"I'm awake already," said Nowacki. Gus winked at him.

"An older woman called Esther did the makeup and rearranged my hair, then we were ready to go."

"Simon, the photographer, said he wanted to work with flash. I didn't think we needed it," said Eunice. "He just wanted to try out a new gadget. I thought it would take simply ages, but he insisted."

"Eunice went first. She told me to watch and began strutting and pouting around the studio," said Milly, turning to Gus. "I thought the little red cocktail dress your Eunice wore looked stunning. It showed off her legs nicely. Maybe it was a bit on the short side, but I didn't like to say anything."

"Then it was Milly's turn," said Eunice. "She's a complete natural, Tunio. After the war, you'll be able to retire on the money she makes. Milly paraded around that studio, sometimes clutching a bouquet of summer blooms or a purse. Simon gave her a pair of dark blue lace gloves, which came halfway up her arms. She was great! We had huge fun, didn't we, Mills?"

"We did. Until..."

"Yes," said Eunice, "until the underwear. I'm afraid Milly baulked at modelling underwear, didn't you?"

"They handed me a pair of satin knickers, which were much too revealing. I refused to put them on."

"Good for you, Milly," said Gus.

"I told her nobody was looking at her bits and to remember that all the men in the room weren't interested in her body at all. Milly blushed, didn't you?"

"I'll say. *Whatever am I getting into?* I thought. I left modelling the underwear to Eunice."

"After the shoot," said Eunice, "I told Simon we were keeping the nylons and he said to keep whatever we liked. So we took the shoes, too. We weren't getting paid, so we had to take what few perks were offered."

"We went to a bar in Soho after the shoot," said Milly. "It was dark and smoky inside. Full of uniformed young men; soldiers and sailors mostly, one or two airmen. Eunice bought us gin and tonics. We sat down at a table by the window and chatted about the shoot. I had fun, but I wasn't sure if I could do it again. I don't have much free time, being in the WAAF, and…"

"And that's when she told me, Tunio. That you and Milly are going to get married."

After the women left, Gus and Nowacki stayed on for more drinks in the mess.

"I tried to tell you sooner," said Nowacki. "Milly's expecting my child and I've asked her to marry me."

"And the bloody war interrupted you," offered Gus.

"I'll ask Staś to be best man. Will you and Eunice come to the wedding? I want all the squadron there."

"Of course, we'll come. We'll be delighted. What about Milly's folks?"

"I think her mother will come along with her younger sister. Harry, her younger brother is away in the Navy. She has an elder brother, Tom, who was wounded at Dunkirk. He'll give her away — that's what you say, isn't it?"

"Yes. That's what we say, but you've got to be sure it's the right thing to do."

"I'm sure it is, Gus. Milly only broke the good news a couple of days ago. I'd gone to see her in Cowley. I went into her room, but she didn't look up, didn't seem pleased to see me. I asked what was wrong. She turned towards me, a tear in her eye, and told me she was pregnant. Well, I couldn't believe it. I flopped down onto the settee and told her it was lovely news. But I could tell she was worried that the child would be born out of wedlock. I jumped up from the settee and knelt down in front of her. I told her I loved her and asked her to marry me. She said I was from another country and that there was a war on. As if I needed reminding."

"Milly may be right, Tunio. Is marrying the right thing to do, for you as well as her? You both have to be sure."

"I love her, Gus. I want to marry her. Baby, war, whatever. I love her. Anyway, she accepted. I told her we'd arrange a wedding as soon as possible. So she said yes and told me that she loved me back. Then she asked how it could work for us."

"How will it work?"

"I told her we could worry about that later. For now, we're young and in love, and she's carrying my baby. That's all that matters."

Later that week, Gus drove the squadron car to Buckinghamshire to visit Squadron Leader Johnson at the Princess Mary's Royal Air Force Hospital in Halton. He took Eunice along for the ride, and they stopped off on the way for a light lunch at a country pub. Then she waited in the car while Gus went into the hospital.

Johnson seemed unusually pleased to see him, but Gus supposed that three weeks of immobility in a hospital bed might make anyone glad of company.

"How are you getting along, sir?" he asked, trying to appear cheerful.

"Fine, fine, thanks. Sit down, Beaumont. How is the squadron?"

"The squadron is coping without you, sir. Squadron Leader Nowacki is doing a sound job in your absence."

"Pah! Now, listen to this, Beaumont. I've got an idea," said Johnson. "I've been chatting with Baker and Smyth-Purse over there." He pointed to two beds, but the occupants had clearly gone elsewhere. "Officers from 12 Group, they are, and they told me how Leigh-Mallory, 12 Group's commander, is up for using Big Wings against the Luftwaffe. His senior officers, including Bader — you know of Bader, don't you?"

"Vaguely," replied Gus.

"Douglas Bader is a friend of mine. He lost both legs in a flying accident but insisted on being a pilot again. Now he's commanding 242 Squadron. He came to see me the other day. He's absolutely convinced that large formations of fighters are essential if we are to defeat the Luftwaffe, and I totally agree with him. We must convince Vice Marshal Park."

"Big Wings? Vice Marshal Park flew Big Wings over Dunkirk, didn't he?" asked Gus.

"Yes, I believe he did," answered Johnson. "Bader was one of the pilots."

"And Park is against the idea now, sir?"

"Park doesn't see the benefits. He only ever sees the dark side of anything. That's always been his problem. Of course, there must be advantages if 12 Group are up for using Big Wings. Think about it, Beaumont: Big Wings will enable us to hit the Germans in very large numbers, which will almost inevitably break up and scatter an attack," explained Johnson. "Bader is going to lead a Big Wing — at least three squadrons of Spitfires and Hurricanes flying and attacking together. It'll be unstoppable! I think Bader's Big Wing could be used as a reserve for 11 Group. Because it's situated well away from the Luftwaffe bases in France, the Wing could be in place at altitude whenever it's needed. Providing adequate early warning is given, of course."

"But without a clear idea of a target, surely it's impossible for a Big Wing to get airborne and form up in time to meet it?"

"Nonsense, Beaumont. Bloody nonsense. You're just as pessimistic as Park. Time for you to go, I think!"

And that was that. Gus walked out of the hospital and got into the car. Eunice seemed strangely quiet on the journey home so Gus did most of the talking, going over the conversation he'd had with Johnson.

"Tell me, why is Vice Marshal Park so against the idea?" asked Eunice.

"He experimented with large groups of fighters to cover the Dunkirk evacuation in May, and he knows the downside of the tactics. The Big Wing is unwieldy, difficult and slow to manoeuvre into position, and rarely in the right place when needed. Wouldn't work for 11 Group."

"Why is that?" asked Eunice.

"For one, 11 Group squadrons are far closer to the Luftwaffe than 12 Group, and that means there isn't enough time. Our radar picks up the attackers, but we don't know where exactly the target is. Kent and Sussex make up too big an area for a very large formation to take off, gain altitude and get into position to fight off the incoming raids. It's better to stick with what we do now — scramble a squadron or even a flight, hit the enemy then return for a quick refuel and rearming, while another squadron from somewhere closer hits them a second time. Hit and run, you might say. Second, the Spitfires have to slow down to keep pace with the Hurricanes. Daft! Let the Spits get there first and attack, then we can hit them later — or pick out the slower bombers."

Once back in north London, Gus dropped Eunice at Chorleywood station so that she could get back to her flat in Hampstead by tube, then he carried on back to Northolt. Nowacki and Staś were waiting in the mess for news.

"How is the old man?" asked Staś.

"He seems to have recovered quite well. Physically, at least. Doctors say the broken leg is mending nicely, though he's hobbling on crutches and will be for a month or so longer."

"He won't be coming home soon, then?"

"Not for a while."

"Good!"

"The problem is, he's in a ward with some chaps from 12 Group. They've been putting crazy ideas into his head about the Big Wing. They seem to have convinced the bugger that we need to switch tactics. I think Grumpy could do more harm confined to the hospital or the office than he possibly could up in the air."

"I met a Czech pilot friend of mine in central London the other day — Dano Jelen," said Nowacki. "He flies Hurricanes with 310 Czech Squadron. He told me a Big Wing has been formed at RAF Duxford."

"Where's that?" asked Staś.

"It's near Cambridge," said Gus. "One of the closest stations to the boundary between 11 and 12 Groups. I'll bet they're going to try to prove Big Wing by operating it from there."

"They have already," said Nowacki. "Dano told me that the Wing was scrambled operationally for the first time a few days ago. It was to patrol North Weald, but the formation arrived too late. He said they were too slow forming up, and for the flight to the patrol area the formation was too disjointed."

"Exactly what Park says and why we in 11 Group don't use the bloody Big Wing," said Gus.

"Dano thinks the Duxford Big Wing isn't at all organised. There's been no rehearsal of how it might work, no planning. He thinks it's just a collection of squadrons led by Bader, who isn't even an experienced squadron leader."

"For such a large formation of fighters to succeed, good planning and lots of training is needed. It sounds like the pilots are getting none of it, from what your Czech friend says."

"It'll never work in any case. Even with training," Nowacki went on. "Dano told me that the deployment of the Wing is always delayed. Bader insists on leading it himself. That means he and his squadron have to fly to Duxford from RAF Coltishall, somewhere up in Norfolk."

"Hold on," said Staś. "Bader wants time to fly to Duxford, land, take off again, then form a Big Wing?"

"Yes," said Nowacki.

"The amount of early warning needed for that! Totally, wildly unrealistic! Just can't be done," said Gus.

"So what do we do?" asked Staś.

"We don't do anything. Grumpy will approach Park and become frustrated when Park won't listen to him. I'll get it in the neck because I always do. Hopefully the idea will go nowhere. It'll just evaporate, given a bit of time."

"Agreed," said Nowacki. "Anyway, we've more pressing issues here, right now."

"Why? What's wrong?" asked Gus.

"The one-hundred-octane fuel is out of stock. We're going back to eighty-seven octane."

"Does it make that much difference?" asked Gus, who hadn't flown a Hurricane on eighty-seven.

"Yes, I'm afraid it does," said Nowacki.

"It causes engine knocking," said Staś.

"Go on."

"The eighty-seven-octane fuel tends to pre-detonate before the completion of the piston compression stroke. This makes the engine less efficient. In practice, the Hurricane's top speed and acceleration both suffer."

"So no tangling with Bf-109s," said Nowacki.

A few days later, Gus received an envelope. It was addressed to him at RAF Sawbridgeworth, his first squadron of Lysanders, and had taken weeks to catch up with him at Northolt. The postmark told him it was from Switzerland. He opened the envelope carefully and found a handwritten letter in French, signed 'M Bachelor'.

That evening, he took the tube to Eunice's flat in Hampstead and asked her to translate.

"Your French is much better than mine," he insisted.

"*Dear Mr Beaumont*," she read aloud. "*I trust this short letter finds you in good health since our previous meeting at the Royal spring flower show. By the way, I think you may have dropped something, and I have it.*

"*I am well. As I predicted, the Old Men caved in. I have moved to a city south of where the Beaujolais meets the Côtes du Rhône and am now actively researching ancestries. If you have the opportunity, you might explain to the Dons that we badly need more tools to carry out the job.* This doesn't make any sense to me, Gus…"

"Just read the bloody thing, Eunice!"

"Hey, calm down, darling," she said, then continued reading. "*By the way, I didn't send anything to Poland lest it might expose a friend — you simply cannot be too careful these days. Yours, M Bachelor.* What on earth does it mean?"

"Well, it helps that I know who it may be from. Professor Marc Bloch — he's an historian. I met him before the war and again at Dunkirk. Look, he signs off as M Bachelor. That's almost an anagram of Marc Bloch, isn't it?"

"Almost, yes."

"Now, 'the Royal spring flower show' — what's that all about? Well, the last time I saw Bloch was aboard a vessel sailing us home from Dunkirk. The *Royal Daffodil* — daffodils are spring flowers."

"So what does this line mean, 'By the way, I think you may have dropped something, and I have it'?" asked Eunice.

"When I was flying Defiants over France —" Gus missed out an essential detail or two — "I dropped a letter to him, asking for it to be posted on to Bloch. Daft thing to do, in retrospect. I could have got somebody into big trouble. I dropped it near a farm, hoping the residents were patriots. Looks like I was lucky. Bloch's telling me he got the note."

"Bloody hell! Clever," said Eunice.

"What's next?"

"*As I predicted, the Old Men caved in,*" she read.

"The French generals and government capitulated. Well, we know that. Next?"

"He says he's moved to a city south of where the Beaujolais meets the Côtes du Rhône and he's researching ancestry. You said he was an historian."

"God! I'm no expert in French wine, so goodness knows where he is. Researching ancestry? What could that be? Read it again, Eunice."

"Actively researching ancestry," she said.

"Ancestry or ancestries? What's the precise translation?"

"Ah, now you mention it, ancestries."

"Another anagram," said Gus. "Ancestries is an anagram of resistance. Exact, this time. Bloch has joined the French Resistance! Now, what's the next bit say?"

"*If you have the opportunity*," read Eunice, "*you might explain to the Dons that we badly need more tools to carry out the job.*"

"Dons. An Oxbridge term he would know, for our teachers…"

"Or elders, those higher up?"

"Yes, he wants me to pass on a message that the Resistance needs guns and bombs, I expect."

"And radios, along with their operator," said Eunice.

Gus looked at her quizzically. "How did you know that?" he asked.

"Bloody obvious! What about the last bit? *By the way, I didn't send anything to Poland lest it might expose a friend — you simply cannot be too careful these days.* What does that mean?"

"I gave him the address of Staś's parents in Poland. Shouldn't have done that, I suppose. Read it back in full again, Eunice. But put in what we think it means."

"*Dear Mr Beaumont, I trust this short letter finds you in good health since our previous meeting aboard the Royal Daffodil. You dropped a letter to me, and I have it. I am well. As I predicted, the French Government and military capitulated to the Nazis. I have moved to a city south of where the Beaujolais meets the Côtes du Rhône and am now active in the French Resistance. If you have the opportunity, you might explain to the British military that we badly need more tools: guns, ammo, radios, agents. By the way, I didn't send anything to Poland lest it might expose Staś's parents — you simply cannot be too careful these days. Yours, Marc Bloch.*"

"Well, I'll be…"

"It's Lyon, by the way," said Eunice.

"What?"

"The city south of where the Beaujolais wine region meets the Côtes du Rhône region. Lyon."

CHAPTER 23

"Scramble! Scramble!" shouted Tunio Nowacki as he sprinted, pulling on his parachute and air vest, towards the parked fighters at the north London base. Staś and Gus followed, chasing the Pole across the grassy strip towards their own Hurricanes. The Polish squadron was quickly airborne and flying to intercept yet another Luftwaffe bombing rain over the capital.

Since the change in Luftwaffe tactics, the Poles had been in the thick of it as, day after day, they fought off hordes of Ju-88s, Do-17s and He-111s. Now, instead of dogfights over the green fields of Kent, Sussex or Surrey, they fought over the offices, houses and churches of central London.

"There they are, six o'clock," called Tunio and the Poles dived onto the bombers and Bf-110 escort fighters of the Luftwaffe.

The German pilots could do nothing as Tunio's Hurricane swept onto a Ju-88 and opened fire on it from what seemed like a suicidally close range. The eight machine guns of the Hurricane spat steel bullets into the fuselage of the Junkers, which pulled slowly to port, fire and thick black smoke streaming from one of its engines.

Gus saw Tunio turn away from the doomed bomber, searching out a second target. The Hurricane was now below a Bf-110, which Gus realised had an advantage. The big, twin-engined fighter went into a shallow dive and accelerated.

"Bandit on your tail, Tunio," Gus called over the RT.

Tunio tried, but was unable to either outpace the Bf-110 or shake it off. The German pilot was gaining on his Hurricane and there was nothing Gus or Staś could do about it — they were too far away and had no height. They could do nothing but look on as the Messerschmitt heavy fighter, one of those with yellow painted propellers and nose, with the white shark's teeth on bright red — this one numbered 3FGH, numbers that became indelibly imprinted onto their brains — opened fire on Tunio's Hurricane.

The shock of the cannon fire ripped apart the fuselage of the British fighter and Tunio wondered whether he would be able to get out of the Hurricane before it either exploded or spun downwards, out of control. He flung back the cockpit cover, quickly unbuckled the webbing straps that held him secure and pushed himself up, out of the seat and clambered onto the starboard wing of the Hurricane.

Gus watched as his friend climbed from the Hurricane's cockpit onto the wing, then rolled off the wing and into the sky. One, two, three seconds then Tunio's parachute opened. As it did, 3FGH came into view having completed a wide turn to aim directly at the defenceless pilot.

Gus looked on in horror as the drama played out in slow motion before his eyes. He saw the bullets rip into Tunio. Saw his body jerk and twitch at the impact of those scores of high-velocity, metal projectiles. Saw it slump, dead, still harnessed to the parachute and now making a slow, directionless decent.

The skirmish over, Gus and the Poles returned to base subdued at the loss of one of their best.

Gus borrowed the squadron car and drove to Cowley, picking up Eunice along the way. They knocked on Milly's door. Her expression as she opened the door and saw them told Gus that nothing much was needed by way of explanation. She invited them in, and they all sat down.

"If it's any consolation, Milly," Gus said, "it was quick. Machine-gun fire. Tunio wouldn't have suffered. We've recovered his body; we can have a funeral and a proper burial."

"Yes," said Milly, as she began sobbing. Eunice held her, and eventually Milly dried her eyes. "I was on duty when it happened. I placed the headphones over my ears and took my place at the map table. Almost immediately, we began to receive news of a large formation of German planes assembling over the Channel and making its way towards the coast. I thought then, as we marked them onto the map, Tunio will have to go up again. What if…?" She paused as fresh tears welled. "Oh, what am I going to do, Eunice? I never thought it could work out for Tunio and me, but…" Milly broke down.

While Eunice stayed by her side, Gus made tea and found some stale biscuits.

"Now I'll be worse off than ever. I'll have to give up my work as a WAAF in a few months, because of the baby. Once I've had it, there'll be nothing for me here. I'll be back up north. Back working at the UCP, probably, but with a baby and then a young child in tow. Oh my God, Eunice. What am I going to do?"

Eunice put her arm around her friend's shoulder. "It'll be all right, Milly. Try not to worry. We still have each other."

Once he was back at the base, Gus quickly found Staś.

"Do you think it was the eighty-seven-octane petrol?" he asked his cousin.

"Well, it won't have helped," Staś replied. He was quiet for a moment and then blurted out, "3FGH is the same bastard that killed Jan Grudziński over Poland."

"You can't be sure."

"I am sure. We know it's the same squadron of Bf-110s. This one flies the same arc as he approaches, opens fire at the same range, and he instinctively banks to starboard when under attack. He's a left hander, 3FGH. We've got to get him, Gus. And when we do, I'm going to kill the murdering Nazi bastard."

"Not if I kill him first," said Gus.

Later that week, Eunice telephoned Gus on the base. He could hear her sobbing.

"Eunice? What's wrong?" he asked, alarmed.

"My parents were killed last night," she wept.

"Don't go anywhere," said Gus. "I'll be with you as soon as I can."

He took the tube to her flat in Hampstead, where she sat him down and told him the whole story.

"Their house was destroyed in the latest bombing raid on London," Eunice explained as she wiped away her tears. "I'd told my parents many times that you said it would be safest for them to move out. Once the Luftwaffe's tactics changed to attacking London rather than the RAF bases around the city, there were bound to be civilian casualties. But they wouldn't listen. My father said there was nothing in Kensington that the Germans would be interested in — he thought they were only after the factories and the docks. If the house were in the East End, well, that would be different. But where he was, he felt safe."

Gus nodded as he took this in. "It was just a horrible twist of fate. The house was probably hit in error by a lone German bomber whose pilot was no doubt lost. I think he simply ditched his bombs and flew back to France."

The facts surrounding the event made no difference to the enormity of the tragedy, of course. Eunice was distraught. Gus poured them gins and made sure Eunice drank a couple, hoping it would help her sleep. Not wanting to leave her on her own, he stayed the night, sleeping on the settee in the lounge.

Gus got himself back to base early the next morning, and the squadron was scrambled almost immediately. Grumpy Johnson was back commanding them, but because he was still on crutches, Staś led the squadron into action.

They flew on an easterly course to intercept a group of bombers who, with their fighter escort, were flying along the Thames estuary towards east London.

Soon after they were airborne, Gus's RT crackled to life. "There should be some Spits from 12 Group with us. They'll take on the fighter escort; our orders are to stop the bombers reaching London or the docks," said Staś.

Ten minutes later, as the Hurricanes were flying over the widening river, Butch Paderewski called out, "Bandits dead ahead!"

"Where are bloody 12 Group?" asked Staś. The skies were empty of any other British fighters. "Looks like we're on our own," he went on. "We'll just have to do the best we can. Yellow section, follow me to distract the fighters. Butch, you lead Red section to attack the bombers. Good hunting!"

Staś led his section of Hurricanes in a wide-angled dive that took them swooping down onto the Bf-109s of the fighter escort. The effect was to disperse the Messerschmitts across the skies over the Thames, leaving Butch Paderewski's section the easier job of attacking the bombers.

Paderewski's swift Hurricanes dived on the Heinkel 111s, immediately hitting two of them and breaking up the formation, rendering their bombs less effective even if the Germans had the opportunity to drop them. Butch had Red section regroup and down they went for a second attack, destroying another Heinkel and sending the rest back home.

The Poles of Yellow section had a much more difficult task on their hands. The Bf-109s had scattered under the impact of Staś's attack, but now there were multiple dogfights in the sky over Essex and the estuary, fights in which the Messerschmitt 109s had a distinct speed advantage over the Hurricanes. The Poles had found out from experience that below about fifteen hundred feet the Hurricane could keep pace with a Bf-109. At higher altitudes, the German fighter had the edge, and what's more, the Poles still had low octane petrol.

Staś, unusually for him, had gone by the book with a classic, out-of-the-sun diving attack on the Bf-109 group, the dive giving the Hurricanes in his section extra speed, but now that advantage was lost. Experienced German pilots were enticing Poles higher into the skies, where the Hurricanes might be more limited. It was every man for himself, and the fighting was fierce.

Staś had a determined Bf-109 on his tail and, try as he might, he couldn't throw it off. Gus, who had himself winged one of the Germans, watched as Staś turned to port, then to starboard with the Bf-109 sticking to him like glue.

"Lower, Staś, you need to go lower!" Gus called over the RT.

Staś responded, taking the Hurricane to within a few feet of the water. Then he made the tightest turn to port that Gus had ever seen, but the German pilot thrust his Messerschmitt into a vertical climb, came over the top and, twisting in the dive, was again on Staś's tail.

Gus dived down to join in. "The weave, Staś! Use Tunio's weave!" he called out over the radio.

Staś quickly adopted a course of tight port and starboard turns at high speed. The Bf-109 followed him. Gus, flying a direct line, closed the distance between them, and as he did, he saw occasional spats of tracer emerging from the guns in the nose of the Messerschmitt. When he felt he was close enough to the two fighters weaving their unsteady course over the Thames, Gus assumed a similar, though not identical course.

Eventually, as he turned to starboard once again, trying to get a clear shot at Staś's Hurricane, the German pilot unwittingly brought his own aircraft fully in front of Gus, who opened up instantly with the eight .303 Browning machine guns mounted along the leading edge of the Hurricane's wings. The shuddering of the guns shook the Hurricane, but Gus held it steady, keeping his finger on the firing button until the Bf-109 burst into flame.

Gus broke off the attack as the Messerschmitt plunged into the dark brown waters of the Thames estuary, steam and smoke filling the now empty air space that the ill-fated fighter once occupied. He looked around for Staś, but Gus couldn't see him anywhere.

Eventually, lack of ammunition or low fuel levels caused the fight to peter out. The German and Polish pilots headed back to base, counting their successes or licking their wounds. When the Poles landed, Staś was missing.

"That German got him," said a young Polish pilot. "A burst of cannon fire took part of Staś's tailplane away. Last I saw of his Hurricane, it had pancaked onto the water. It went down quickly after that. One second it was there, the next it had disappeared."

"Did you see if Staś got out before the plane sank?" asked Gus.

"Couldn't tell, sorry, Bouncer. Had a Nazi on my tail."

"Not your fault," said a dejected Gus.

"Shit! It's that bloody eighty-seven-octane petrol," said Gus as he walked from the office with Butch Paderewski. "Staś couldn't pull away from the Jerry; it must be the petrol that's to blame."

The pilots each put in their reports. Red section had claimed two Bf-109s down with the loss of Staś. Yellow had downed two Heinkel 111s and damaged three others. No German bombs from that raid had landed on British soil. All in all, it counted as a good sortie for the Polish squadron, but Gus was unhappy.

"First, we lost Tunio. Yesterday my girlfriend's parents were killed by the Germans, and now my cousin is shot down and missing. Bad news always comes in threes, doesn't it?"

"Chin up, Bouncer," said Butch. "He'll be fine, you just wait."

Bad news might traditionally come in threes, but the following day brought double good news to the Poles.

First, Staś Rosen arrived, uninjured, back at the base. He'd been picked up by an RAF rescue boat and, apart from being slightly hypothermic following his swim in the estuary, he was in fine fettle and keen to get back into an aeroplane. Then, just hours after Staś's return, two fuel tankers arrived at the base and they were both brim-full of one-hundred-octane petrol.

CHAPTER 24

Tunio Nowacki and Eunice Hesketh's parents were buried within a day of each other. Afterwards, Gus managed to wangle some leave and he took Eunice by train from Waterloo to Winchester for a weekend break. His family's gleaming black Austin Windsor saloon was waiting for them outside Winchester station. The chauffeur, Albert, was standing beside it, just as he had the previous summer.

"Good afternoon, Mr Beaumont. Very good to see you back."

"Hello, Albert. Nice to see you again. Remember Miss Hesketh?"

"Afternoon, Miss," said Albert with a smile as he closed the car door behind Gus.

Albert drove them to Gus's family home. They walked in to find Magda sitting alone in the morning room, the curtains partly closed to keep out the sunshine.

"Mother," said Gus, "lovely to see you. You're looking very well. You remember Eunice Hesketh; she visited a few years ago. We were both at Oxford."

"Do I? Well, good afternoon, Miss Hesketh. Do sit down. Are you staying?"

"For the weekend," said Gus. "I wrote to you, remember?"

"Did you?"

"Yes. And why the closed curtains, Mother?"

Gus got to his feet and walked over to the windows. He drew back the drapes, allowing the sun to flood the room. In the light, he could see the drawn look on his mother's face. Her eyes were red, with dark shadows under them, and she had obviously lost weight. He glanced at Eunice, who nodded knowingly.

After a late lunch, they took a couple of bicycles from the shed and rode over to Oliver's Battery, a giant old earthwork on the western side of the city.

"The archaeologists think it was Iron Age," explained Gus as the couple strolled around the ancient remains.

"Then why is it called Oliver's?"

"The name dates back to the English Civil War. It's associated with Oliver Cromwell's siege of Winchester in 1645. But I'm pretty sure cannon fire of that period wouldn't have had the range to fire on Winchester, so I doubt it was an actual battery. More likely a camp. I've seen old maps in the museum that call it Cromwell's Camp, and I suppose the earthworks may well have provided a suitable campsite for the besieging Parliamentarian forces," he explained. "There was an army camp here during the Great War. The army had a large veterinary hospital for horses here, too. See the huts over there?" He pointed to a small group of ex-army huts.

"Yes."

"After the war, the camp was split up into smallholdings. The huts are used as dwellings now."

"Must be cold in the winter," she said.

"And I doubt they're properly waterproof," mused Gus.

"We just don't know how lucky we are, do we? There's so much inequality, even in England, one of the richest countries in the world," said Eunice. "And so much evil!"

They got back onto their bicycles and carried on to Hursley. The village was bustling with traffic, some of it military. Scores of people, mostly men, were milling around the place, smoking, chatting, or drinking pints of beer at the village pub.

"I thought we might go in for a drink," said Gus, "but it looks too busy."

"It doesn't look that large a village. Why are there so many people around?"

"It's because of Hursley Park and the house. The boffins and engineers from Supermarine are based there; it's safer than Southampton. I expect they're working on new ideas and developments for the Spitfires. Shall we have a drink? What do you think?"

"Let's go back," said Eunice.

That evening, dinner was eaten almost silently. Magda hardly said a word, nor did she eat very much. Then she decided it was time for bed at about eight thirty, leaving Gus and Eunice alone.

"She's not well," said Eunice.

"Clearly."

"Depressed?"

"Probably. I'll need to have a word with Doctor Harris, but I can't do it tomorrow. I'll try to phone him on Monday. It's a shame — I wanted to talk to her."

"About what?"

"Her past. Something's been bothering me for quite a while now."

"Can you tell me?" asked Eunice.

"Not tonight," he replied. "Tomorrow, we'll see if she'll talk to us about it."

"I'm ready for bed," said Eunice, standing. "It's been a long day, with all that cycling around!"

"But you did enjoy it?"

"Yes, Gus, of course I did." She went over to him, smiled, then kissed him on the lips. "Good night, darling," she said, then went upstairs to her bedroom on the first floor.

Gus poured himself a whisky, then sat down and pondered.

Magda seemed brighter the next morning, and Gus thought seeing him and Eunice might have lifted her mood. She refused to go to church, so after breakfast the three of them settled in the morning room for coffees.

"Father told me of your friendship with Rosa Luxemburg. I'm intrigued."

"Rosa. Yes, such a long time ago."

"She was a communist, wasn't she?"

"Rosa was everything! You are familiar with the term 'Renaissance man'? Well, Rosa was enlightenment woman! She studied philosophy, history, politics, economics, and mathematics in Zurich. She specialised in political science, economic and stock exchange crises, and the Middle Ages, and she wrote a doctoral thesis on the industrialisation of Poland. That made her one of the first women in the world with a doctorate in economics."

"She sounds wonderful," said Eunice, "to achieve so much in a world where the odds are stacked against women."

"True," said Magda, "especially when you know she was dead before she was fifty."

"Tell me more about her politics, Mother."

"Rosa was a socialist. Later she became a Spartacist. Perhaps she was a communist, too — she certainly read much of Karl Marx's work. But before anything, she was a nationalist — a Polish nationalist. It's difficult for you youngsters to appreciate. These days, nationalism is such a dirty word, with these right-wing nationalists in Germany, Italy and Japan. But in the days when the Russian Tsars ruled over Poland, many of us were nationalists."

"I can understand that," said Gus.

"Rosa was different to many, because she believed that the struggle should be against capitalism, not just for Polish independence. She thought an independent Poland could only come about through socialist revolutions in Germany, Austria-Hungary and Russia. That's why she moved to Germany, to be part of a socialist revolution there, to provoke one, even. That's why she and the others formed the Spartacist League during the last war. That's why she was murdered!"

"That's interesting," said Gus. "So, would you say that for Rosa, communism was a means to an end? To liberate Poland and create an independent nation?"

"Socialism, not communism, was both a means and the end. She saw the misery that poverty brought to so many in Poland, Germany and elsewhere. Socialism was necessary to end that. An independent Poland was a means of combatting the imperialism and capitalism that exploited the Polish working class."

"We have the same levels of poverty here too, Mrs Beaumont. Gus and I saw those hovels over by Oliver's Battery yesterday, and I've seen it in London — in the slums around the East End and other parts of the city. My friend Milly is a working-class woman from the north. She's told me tales of how her family and friends suffered during the Great Depression. It's awful. And look at me — I want for nothing in any material sense. Yet, I don't work for it. It all seems so horribly unbalanced and unfair."

"That's what capitalism does, Miss Hesketh. It is a system that works by exploitation. It exploits the land for resources and exploits people by using their labour at the lowest rate of pay possible. Simple economics. But, Gustaw, why are you so interested to know if Rosa Luxemburg was a communist or not? Does it really matter?"

"Well, because communism is a…"

"A dirty word?" asked Magda. "Do you think that because Stalin has corrupted Marx's ideal, communists are wicked? Is that it?"

"Well, I'm not sure…"

"Who stood up to Hitler before 1933, Gus?" asked Magda. "Who was it that fought against Hitler's Brown Shirts in the streets of Berlin and Munich? Was it the liberals? The social democrats? No! It was the communists. Think about it, both Hitler and Mussolini had to eliminate the left in their countries before they took on the liberals. It's not bad to be a communist, is it?"

"Do you think there will be a communist movement here in England, Mrs Beaumont?"

"Unlikely, I'd say. There was a chance, of course, when that dreadful Oswald Mosely's thugs were on the streets. They managed to unite the left and politicised most Jews. But Hitler's success in France has done for the British Fascists; I read somewhere that Mosely is in Holloway Prison. His wife, too!"

"Oh, really? I didn't know that."

"We have the Labour Party," she continued. "Of course, they're social democrats, not proper socialists. This war has done them a great favour. They are now part of Churchill's National Government. Attlee, Bevin and Greenwood are Cabinet members, and I read in the newspapers that Labour's Ellen Wilkinson — now she *is* left-wing — has been appointed a Parliamentary Secretary. They might even form a government after the war. If Britain wins it, of course."

"If we don't win it, we won't have a say in who governs us," said Eunice.

Magda nodded.

"A very bright chap called Harold Wilson was in some of my classes at Oxford," said Gus. "He's Labour and says he wants to become an MP. I'd certainly vote for him!"

"Do I detect that your liberalism might be turning a little more to the left, Gustaw?" asked his mother.

"I suppose it must."

"Goodness me!" said Magda. "All this talk about politics has worn me out. But I have enjoyed chatting with you. Look, I'm tired. I want to take a nap. What will you two do?"

"I think we'll just take a stroll around town," said Gus, "and we'll have to be on our way back to London directly after tea. If that's all right with you?"

"Of course, it is. I understand — you've a war to fight. Listen, Gustaw, listen carefully. You must promise never to allow any feelings of duty towards me to get in the way of what you want to do! Never, understand?"

"Yes, Mother."

"You promise?"

"I promise."

"Then off you go, you two," said Magda. "As I said, you've a war to fight!"

Gus looked at Eunice and wondered where this war would lead them.

A few days after they had returned from Winchester, Gus visited Eunice at her flat and knew at once that something wasn't as it should be. Eunice was clearly hiding something from him.

"What's the matter?" he asked.

"Sit down, Gus," said Eunice. "I've got something to tell you."

He sat down on the settee.

"I'm sorry, Gus, but I have to go away, probably for a long time."

He had thought this was coming. She had been becoming more and more distant. This had happened once before, in Oxford, when Eunice had tried to explain to him that things were wrong, that it would never 'work out' for them. Now it was happening again. Were things getting too serious? Was she about to finish with him for a second time? Was it even worth trying to find out why she was leaving?

"It's not because of us," she said. "It's the war. I have to do something; I simply must. I was on the train after our outing in Halton — do you remember? When you went to see your squadron leader in the hospital there?"

"Of course I remember."

"My mind wandered, and I realised how envious I was of Milly, working as a WAAF. I was dwelling on how bored I was with my comfortable lifestyle, living in the flat, doing some occasional modelling, seeing you. Then an RAF officer sat down opposite me. He looked remarkably handsome in his smart uniform. He reminded me of you. I like you, Gus, of course, but… I began to think of Xavier — remember I told you about…"

"I remember."

"I wondered, was he still in France? The northern part is now occupied by the Germans, and the rest is a compliant state run by a puppet government in Vichy. Was Xavier resisting? Was he alive? Then you showed me the letter from your friend Bloch. I felt that I really must do something. I gazed out of the carriage window at the tightly packed houses of north London, wondering what might become of them. You and Milly had told me that the Luftwaffe had switched to attacking the factories and houses of London rather than the

RAF bases. Well, what could I do? Just what could I do? The Land Army…"

"Not you, Eunice."

"No, but maybe I could become a WAAF, like Milly…"

"Well, you'd look nice in that uniform…"

"And now I've found something, Gus. I went to see Sir Alexander Peacock again."

"Eunice! You didn't! You can't!"

"I did. I met him in a pub out in Rickmansworth. It was rather dark inside, as some country pubs tend to be. Peacock was standing at the bar, dressed in civilian clothing."

"That's unusual, for him. What did he have to say?"

"He greeted me gushingly and offered me a Kir Royale, but I asked for a glass of water instead."

"How very unsophisticated — not like you," said Gus.

"I needed a clear head. Peacock asked me why I wanted to meet him, but I wasn't ready to say. Not yet. I asked why he had me come here, to Rickmansworth of all places. He said it was just a simple rule he tries to keep. If Peacock doesn't call the meeting and doesn't know what it's about, he always chooses the territory."

"He needs to be in control, you see," said Gus. "I can guess what you wanted to talk to him about. Was it something to do with the offer he made you all those months ago? To join his special agents?"

"Yes."

"And?"

"Peacock had said I should get onto him when I'd thought it through. I told him I had and asked if the offer was still available. He said the short answer was yes, and asked when I could start the training. I told him I wasn't doing much else at the moment. So he said he'd find out when the next course starts and get back to me. Then he said I should remember it was absolutely top secret and warned me not to breathe a word to anyone. But now I've told you, Gus."

"Yes, you have."

"Look, I'm sorry, Gus. I'm not supposed to discuss it — careless talk costs lives, you know. But I had to tell you. I couldn't just leave, could I? But it's terribly hush-hush. I might be parachuting into France one day."

"Bloody hell, Eunice!" Gus stared at her; her hair was just as golden as it always had been, her lips just as red. "I understand," he lied, desperately trying to imagine Eunice leaving him to fight a secret war in a foreign country where she probably would be killed. "You have to do it if you feel it's the right thing. I suppose I should go now."

"Yes," she said, "but don't go yet. Stay with me a while."

Eunice placed a disc onto the record player and undressed, slowly and seductively. Then, more urgently, she began to undress Gus, and they made love to the sound of Glenn Miller's 'Moonlight Serenade'.

CHAPTER 25

"Post for you, Staś," said Gus, rushing back to the mess from the ward office.

"Post for me?"

"It's from Poland. Here."

Staś's face was frozen. Gus could only imagine his cousin's apprehension. Letters from an occupied country on the other side of Europe were unusual, and there were two envelopes for Staś. It couldn't be good news.

Staś looked at the small package. "It's been processed by someone. Probably some clerk at an RAF headquarters," he said, removing the elastic band and taking out the note. "Getting anything out of Poland is a bloody miracle. Has your contact Peacock had anything to do with it? This note is signed by Piotr Krawiec."

"Nothing to do with me, Staś. Honest."

Gus could see that one of the notes had been neatly written by hand. The other was typed. Staś looked at the handwritten one first, reading quickly. He turned to Gus. "It's from a neighbour of my parents, Tanya — she's not Jewish. But she writes about the fate of Polish Jews and how she lost contact with my parents. Listen to this: *They have been taken away to a concentration camp in Oświęcim, near Kraków. It was opened in June and the Germans call it Auschwitz. I don't know if they were moved there because they are Polish resistance activists — most of the prisoners are. Or perhaps it's just because they are Jews. But Staś, be prepared. Nobody comes out of those camps.*"

"When is it dated?"

"April this year."

"Six months ago," said Gus.

Quickly, Staś took the second note. "My God," he said. He was shaking as he dropped the letter on the floor. Gus reached for it. It was typed and unsigned, but Gus worked out that it purportedly came from the *Związek Walki Zbrojnej*, the Polish underground. Dated August 1940, the note had clearly been rushed through whatever secret means of communicating with the free world the Poles of *Związek Walki Zbrojnej* still had. The note was brief, curtly informing Staś that his parents were believed to be dead.

"I'm so, so sorry, Staś," said Gus softly.

Sporting a filthy hangover brought on by commiserating too heavily with his cousin, Gus made his way to Gravesend by train the next day. The night fighter squadron, still flying Defiants, was now based at RAF Gravesend, and Gus had found out that his old friend from his training days, Stewart Poore, had been posted to it.

On the way, he was going to meet Sir Alexander Peacock at the RAF Club. The summer before, London had been all sandbags and nervousness over the impending war. Now there were still sandbags almost everywhere he looked, but there were bombsites as well. The mood was somehow different too: stoic and determined. He found the club, entered and asked for Peacock. Soon the officer appeared.

"Nice to see you again, Gustaw," said Peacock. "What can I do for you, old boy?"

"I was passing through on my way to Kent and just wondered if any progress had been made with the secret operations? You know, the Lysander drops."

"Still a long way off, Gustaw. A long way off. Tell me, are you interested?"

"Yes, I'd like to have a bash at it."

"Well, listen. When the time comes, I'll certainly keep you in mind. But I may have another job for you to do first."

He wondered what adventure the old man might have in mind for him next. Would he be able to resist it?

"Tell me about it," said Gus.

"I can't say too much, not until I know you're definitely on board. But it will mean getting a posting to somewhere in the Mediterranean. Greece, maybe. Or Palestine, or perhaps Egypt."

Gus hesitated. Eunice was still dominating his thoughts, but whatever she was getting herself mixed up in would surely take her away from him — at least for the duration of the war. There was nothing to keep him here in England; his mother had made it clear that he must do what he felt was best for himself.

"Yes," he said, "you can count me in."

"Good man, Beaumont," said Peacock. "I'll be in touch — when the time comes. Shouldn't be too long."

Gus left the RAF Club and ate a spot of lunch in a café on Tottenham Court Road. The sedate swing music of Glenn Miller filled the dining room. *Please, oh please, don't play 'Moonlight Serenade'*, he thought. Afterwards, he made his way to Charing Cross and caught the train to Gravesend. From the carriage windows he gazed out over the ruined streets and factories of east London, testament to the Luftwaffe's switch to bombing civilian targets. *Bastards*, he thought.

Once he'd arrived in Gravesend, Gus met Stewart Poore at a pub in town.

"Great to see you, Bouncer," Poore greeted.

"How's the old squadron going, Poorly?" Gus asked.

"Oh, much better since you left," he laughed. "Some of the boys you know are still there. Keats is in hospital. Pine Marten's the acting squadron leader."

"What happened to Keats?"

"He was badly burnt," said Poore. "His Daffy got into a bit of a scrap. Jerry has started using Bf-110s as night intruders. They fly over with the bomber formations then split off and try to shoot us down when we're taking off or landing. Devious bastards, aren't they?"

"What about the rear gunner, Poorly? Did he make it?"

"Sadly not."

"Who was it?"

Poore hesitated. "It was Spud Murphy. Sorry, Bouncer."

"What happened?"

"It was a night operation over the Thames estuary. The crew of one of the other planes saw it all, from a distance. Keats and Spud brought down a Messerschmitt but got shot up in the process. A fuel tank was hit. Keats did the right thing in ordering a bail-out. He made it with bad burns, but the Defiant burst into flames and Spud couldn't get out of the bloody turret. He burned to death up there."

"Spud always feared that," said Gus.

"That's what all rear gunners fear," replied Poore.

When Gus was back in Northolt and sitting in his room, he reflected on what had happened over the past few months. The deaths of Tunio Nowacki and Spud Murphy had shaken him. What a price they had paid for resisting the Nazis. And poor Milly Turner had been left to raise a baby on her own — a child who would never know its father. Eunice's parents were dead too. What was Eunice doing now? Was she safe? He gave himself a mental shake. Did he care what Eunice was doing? Was she good for him?

Then he remembered that he still had Bunty Kermode's address in the breast pocket of his uniform tunic. *God, I'm so bloody mixed up*, he thought. *The sooner Peacock gets back to me, the better!*

CHAPTER 26

The following morning, German aircraft were detected and the squadron scrambled. As they flew towards the enemy, Gus's heart pounded as he spotted a familiar plane.

"Staś!" he said over the RT. "It's him! I'm sure of it."

He looked again at the group of Bf-110s above them. Overall, they were painted in the standard green camouflage of the Luftwaffe, and he could see the black crosses on the underwings. Their noses and the two engine cowlings were picked out in a garish, bright yellow, and beneath the noses were shark's teeth, highlighted in white on red. On the lead aircraft, he could just make out the number, 3FGH. Yes, it was him. Nowacki's killer.

Gus felt his agitation rising. The deaths of Eunice's parents, his Polish aunt and uncle, and the murder of Tunio Nowacki had each had a profound effect on him. He probably should have been grounded for a week or two, but with so many of the Poles gone, he knew that the squadron needed him more than ever. He and Staś were by far the most experienced pilots remaining.

Gus forced his mind back to the present. There were six Hurricanes in the flight, flying in three pairs. Gus was Staś's wingman. The Poles knew from their combat experience that the Bf-110s were too heavy to dogfight successfully, and too cumbersome to mix with the faster and nimbler Hurricanes. In a one-on-one dogfight, the Hurricane would win. But height and momentum were always advantages and, in practice, the pilots that spotted the enemy first and were able to attack generally got better results.

"Break off in pairs!" called Staś. "Max to port, Jerzy starboard. We carry on straight ahead, Gus."

The Hurricanes to their left and right peeled away, taking two of the Messerschmitts with them. As one of the German pilots opened fire, Max Bartoszyn's wingman was caught in a hail of bullets and cannon fire. His Hurricane began to smoke badly then spin downwards, out of control. Max, meanwhile, was trying to gain height so that he might attack the Bf-110 that had shot down his wingman.

Over on the right-hand side of the fight, the pair of Hurricanes led by Jerzy Filipek were outpacing the Bf-110 on their tails. *Thank goodness for the one-hundred-octane petrol*, thought Gus.

Staś and Gus were being chased by the other two Bf-110s. One of these was 3FGH. *Good*, thought Gus, *but how to get above or behind them?* The answer soon came to him. "Go to port, Staś!" he called over the RT, simultaneously putting his own Hurricane into a very tight turn in the opposite direction.

The Bf-110s couldn't match the Hurricanes, but continued their dive nevertheless. As two of the German pilots began a slow climb, Staś and Gus climbed faster, heading towards the sun. Jerzy and the other Hurricane were nowhere to be seen. *No matter*, thought Gus. He and Staś were now above the killer in 3FGH and the other Bf-110, still trying to link up with the rest of their group.

"Ready, Gus?"

"Ready."

"Follow me. Tally-ho!"

"Roger, wilco."

The two Hurricanes entered into a steep dive, emerging from the sun and sweeping onto the unsuspecting Bf-110s.

One of the German pilots fired a long burst towards Staś. The range was too far to do any damage, however, and Gus knew the seventy-five rounds would expire after about four seconds and the German rear gunner would have to reload his weapon. This offered a brief opportunity for Staś to attack with impunity.

The gunfire paused. Staś opened the throttle even further, closed in on the nearest Bf-110 and opened fire with the eight Brownings in the Hurricane's wings. Gus almost felt the vibration of the fire, which shook Staś's Hurricane. Nevertheless, Staś closed in even further, only rolling away at the last moment. As he did so, Gus saw the rear cockpit canopy of 3FGH turn red.

"Rear gunner hit!" he called over the RT.

"Roger that. Your turn, Gus. Remember, he's likely to bank to starboard."

The second Bf-110 had managed to peel off, and Gus saw it in the far distance heading south. Now it was his turn to attack 3FGH. As Gus turned and climbed, lining up his approach, he hoped and prayed that Staś would now be acting as his wingman and looking out for any other German aircraft.

Still in a dive, Gus quickly gained on the Bf-110, holding his fire until the range was so close that his machine gun would destroy the German plane. No fire greeted him. His cousin had done a good job; the German rear gunner was either dead or so badly injured he could do nothing.

3FGH was defenceless. Gus's Hurricane was gaining on it, and the German pilot could neither outmanoeuvre nor outpace him. At two hundred feet, Gus opened fire. 3FGH banked to starboard, but Gus predicted the move and kept it in his gun sight. He opened with a second burst of fire, the effect of which was devastating on the defenceless German plane.

Bullets rained into the tailplane and wings, causing the pilot to lose control. Gus watched him as he thrust back the cockpit canopy and unclipped his straps. As the Hurricane sped by, the German pilot rolled out of his cockpit and slid off the rear of the wing into the air.

The parachute opened, jerking the pilot's body as it slowed him down to a gentle fall. There was little wind, and Gus looked down as the pilot floated towards the green fields below him.

As Gus watched the man, he remembered Tunio Nowacki's fate. Good old Tunio, probably the best pilot of them all. Tunio, who had fought the Germans in Poland, France and here in the skies over England. Tunio, who'd saved the lives of the Wellington bomber's crew by bravely climbing out onto the flaming wing, only to be butchered by this evil Nazi pilot. He thought of Milly Turner carrying his child. Then he thought of Eunice's parents, Flight Sergeant Bernard Chester — the first of his comrades to die — and Spud Murphy. His anger rose.

Gus aimed his Hurricane at the German and closed the range. Now was the time.

He flew closer and closer but rolled away at the last minute. No, he couldn't shoot at a defenceless airman, no matter what. What was it Nowacki had said? *Ah, yes,* Gus thought. *We are both officers and gentlemen.*

The German pilot descended almost gracefully as Gus gained height. Staś was circling overhead, scanning the skies for enemy planes. There was nothing.

"They seem to have gone away, Gus," he radioed.

"Roger. How's your fuel gauge?"

"Getting low. We'll return to base," ordered Staś. Gus looked down at his compass and picked a course for base. As he did so, he glimpsed Staś still circling over the German pilot.

"You have to report me," said Staś once he and Gus were back at the base and sitting in the mess.

"Report you? For what?" asked Gus.

"I attacked that German pilot that bailed out. It must be against the Geneva Convention or something, but I couldn't help it. I looked at the yellow nose and shark's teeth painted onto 3FGH, and I remembered the machine-gun fire that had ripped into Jan Grudziński. I thought of my parents' suffering, their deaths in that Nazi concentration camp. I thought of all the other Jews who have been murdered, and the Poles rounded up and hung by the Nazis for their brave resistance. I remembered Tunio's body hanging from the parachute, the bullets from 3FGH pumping into it and making it jerk like a puppet on a string. Then I lost control. I lost any compassionate or honourable principles I ever had, Gus. I blasted a defenceless pilot to pieces. You should report me."

"Forget it, Staś," said Gus. "We know he was a murdering Nazi bastard. He deserved what he got."

HISTORICAL NOTES

CHARACTERS AND PERSONALITIES

Wing Commander Sir Alexander Peacock is entirely fictitious, though I expect military types like him were scattered all over wartime London. Reading between the lines, Peacock is recruiting both Gus Beaumont and Eunice Hesketh for service in what became the Special Operations Executive (SOE). The SOE was formed in 1940 from the amalgamation of three existing secret organisations (MI6, the Electra House Department, and MI(R), the guerrilla warfare research department of the War Office). The purpose of the SOE was to conduct reconnaissance, espionage and sabotage against the Axis powers in occupied Europe, and to aid local resistance movements. Peacock both forms and haunts Bouncer's RAF career; he and the SOE are to re-appear in future stories.

I have based Lieutenant Duncan Farquhar on Airey Neave. Neave was involved in the defence of Calais in 1940 and was captured by the Germans. He escaped from Colditz Castle — a high security POW camp for officers who had become security or escape risks or who were regarded by the Germans as particularly dangerous. See *Flames of Calais: A Soldier's Battle* by Airey Neave (Hodder & Stoughton, 1972).

The seemingly unlikely story of Tunio Nowacki's exploits on the wing of a Wellington Bomber is based on fact. Sergeant James Allen Ward of 75 (New Zealand) Squadron extinguished a fire in the engine of a Vickers Wellington bomber flying over occupied Europe on the night of 7/8th July 1941, for which he was awarded not a DFC, but the Victoria Cross.

Air Chief Marshal Sir Hugh Caswall Tremenheere (Stuffy) Dowding, 1st Baron Dowding, GCB, GCVO, CMG (1882–1970) was head of RAF Fighter Command during the Battle of Britain and is generally credited with playing a crucial role in Britain's defence, and hence the defeat of Adolf Hitler's plan to invade Britain. He was knighted in 1937.

Marc Bloch (1886–1944) and Lucien Febvre founded the Annales School of 'total history' in 1919. Bloch fought against the Nazis in 1940 and wrote about the fall of France in his book, *Strange Defeat* (Oxford University Press, 1949) some of which I used in constructing his account to Gus on board the *Royal Daffodil.* Having been evacuated from Dunkirk, Bloch went by train to Plymouth and over to Brittany to fight on. After the defeat of France, he fought with the French Resistance. He appears in future Gus Beaumont Aviation Thrillers, so I shan't say more about him here.

PLACES

The French showed much faith in their magnificent and expensive Maginot Line. The German attack of May 1940 bypassed the defensive line, leading to the fall of France and Dunkirk (also covered by Bloch's book).

Hursley Park near Winchester had been a military camp in 1914–18. In early 1940 Sir George Cooper died, leaving his elderly wife alone with her servants. She volunteered the house to be used as a hospital. Air raids on Southampton forced the requisition of the house, not for a hospital, but to safely house the designers and production management of Supermarine. Later in the war, Hursley was at the very heart of the D-Day preparations with the British 50th (Northumbrian) Division based in the two camps in the park.

AIRCRAFT AND TACTICS

Much has been written, and posted on the internet, about the relative merits of the Hawker Hurricane, Supermarine Spitfire and Messerschmitt Bf-109. Having considered much of this, I have come to the conclusion that these were by far the three best single-engine fighter aircraft of the first couple of years of the Second World War. They are so closely matched in terms of performance and firepower that any advantages were probably ironed out by tactics and pilot skill/experience.

The Messerschmitt Bf-110, on the other hand, Göring's *Eisenseiten* (Ironsides), whilst successful in Poland and France, had a much more difficult job as an escort fighter when it encountered Hurricanes and Spitfires in numbers. Bf-110s served well on the Russian Front and in other combat roles (for example, as light bombers and night fighters) later in the war.

There is much detail of the battles against the Luftwaffe in Poland and the escape of Polish forces to fight in France and England in *For Your Freedom and Ours: The Kościuszko Squadron: Forgotten Heroes of World War II* by Lynne Olson and Stanley Cloud (Arrow Books, 2004).

Many Poles fought with Britain and its Allies in the war and there were a number of Polish fighter squadrons active with the RAF in 1940: 303 Squadron based at RAF Northolt is perhaps the most well-known and widely written about (see *For Your Freedom and Ours*).

The weave tactic that Tunio Nowacki explains to Gus is actually the Thach Weave (also known as a beam defence position), an aerial combat tactic developed by US Navy pilot John S. Thach. It was a tactic designed to combat the superior speed and manoeuvrability of the Japanese Mitsubishi A6M

Zero fighter encountered by Grumman F4F Wildcats.

There remains controversy surrounding the role of Douglas Bader's Duxford Big Wing. The Wing was mobilised during the Battle of Britain and casualties were significantly lower than they were for smaller formations, which suggests that it benefited from protection in numbers. But the Big Wing invariably joined combat with the enemy over northern London, where the German fighter escort was at the very limit of its range and effectiveness. On balance, Air Vice Marshal Sir Keith Park's tactics, which included the occasional use of two and three squadron wings, seem to have been largely appropriate for the conditions 11 Group had to fight under.

The women flyers of the Air Transport Auxiliary are some of the unsung heroes of the war. The Air Transport Auxiliary was a civilian organisation set up to ferry new, repaired, and damaged military aircraft between factories, assembly plants, maintenance depots and active service squadrons and airfields. The pilots also transported service personnel on urgent duty and carried out some air ambulance work. Winnie Crossley was the first female ATA pilot to be checked out on a Hurricane fighter, in July 1941, so Bunty Kermode's delivery flight is almost a year too early.

A NOTE TO THE READER

Dear Reader.

Thank you for taking the time to read *Bouncer's Battle*. I hope you enjoyed reading it as much as I enjoyed writing it.

Reviews are invaluable to authors, so if you liked the book, I'd be grateful if you could leave a review on **Amazon** or **Goodreads**.

Readers can connect with me online **on Facebook** and **X (formerly Twitter)**.

I hope we meet again in Gus Beaumont's next adventure!

Tony Rea

SAPERE
BOOKS